SUMMER OF ENCHANTMENT

SUMMER OF ENCHANTMENT

Julie Coffin

Chivers Press • G.K. Hall & Co.
Bath, England   Thorndike, Maine USA

This Large Print edition is published by Chivers Press, England, and by G.K. Hall & Co., USA.

Published in 1999 in the U.K. by arrangement with the author.

Published in 1999 in the U.S. by arrangement with Julie Coffin.

U.K. Hardcover   ISBN 0-7540-3731-2   (Chivers Large Print)
U.K. Softcover   ISBN 0-7540-3732-0   (Camden Large Print)
U.S. Softcover   ISBN 0-7838-8574-1   (Nightingale Series Edition)

The text of this Large Print edition is unabridged.
Other aspects of the book may vary from the original edition.

Set in 16 pt. New Times Roman.

Printed in Great Britain on acid-free paper.

British Library Cataloguing in Publication Data available

Library of Congress Cataloging-in-Publication Data

Coffin, Julie.
    Summer of enchantment / by Julie Coffin.
        p.   cm.
    ISBN 0-7838-8574-1 (lg. print : sc : alk. paper)
    1. Large type books.   I. Title.
    [PR6053.O3S86   1999]
    823'.914—dc21   99–19634

CHAPTER ONE

Wreckers' Cove. From the name she'd imagined it would be rather a bleak, sinister place, but as the taxi began to wind its way down through a collection of whitewashed and greystone cottages, Lisa caught a glimpse of the sea, all soft blues and greens, a pale curve of sandy beach and high, brown granite cliffs dappled by late afternoon sunshine.

It looked remote and peaceful. Maybe here she could find contentment.

'That's the old 'Mermaid', m'dear.' The driver's rich Cornish voice broke into her thoughts.

Turning a final twist in the lane, the car stopped in front of an old stone building leaning slightly away from the edge of the sea.

'Gwen!' he called out loudly, carrying her suitcase through the open doorway of the inn, 'it's the new young lady . . . from London.'

The room seemed dark after the sharp brightness of the sun and it took a moment or two for Lisa's grey eyes to adjust, before taking in the comfy armchairs and sofas covered in a deep-red flower-patterned William Morris chintz, and the soft glow of the polished wooden floor scattered with faded Persian rugs. The kind of room to make you feel welcome, she decided.

1

A door opened somewhere out of sight and a smell of baking drifted into the air. Then footsteps echoed along a passage and a tall, slender woman came in.

'Scones,' she said with an apologetic smile, brushing a curl of fly-away grey hair from her face with one floury hand. 'Had to pop them in the oven first. Hello, Lisa, my dear. I'm Gwen Pendeen, and delighted to meet you. I expect you're dying for a cup of tea after that long train journey. Have you time for one as well, Tom? Let's all go through to the kitchen, shall we?'

She led the way along a low-ceilinged, wooden-floored corridor, and a comforting fragrant warmth surrounded Lisa as she sat down at a long wooden table. A mixing bowl and rolling-pin were whisked away into the deep sink to be replaced by a pretty blue pottery teapot and matching mugs.

'Just a quick cup, Gwen, m'dear. I've to take Sam Tulliver over to Tehidy to visit Mary in hospital shortly,' Tom said, then glanced round. 'Where's young Jamie today?'

Gwen Pendeen pointed through the salt-hazed window to where a small fair-haired boy knelt on one of the white-painted metal chairs at a round table on the patio outside, deeply engrossed in the picture he was drawing.

'Jamie's my grandson,' she explained to Lisa, and her face fell slightly. 'He lives here. My son's divorced, you see.'

She turned back to the window again. 'Always drawing, that child.'

'Takes after your Matthew then. Maybe you're going to have two architects in the family.' Tom chuckled, drinking up the tea and with a nod in Lisa's direction, he rose to his feet again. 'Settle in well, m'dear, though with Gwen here to look after you, t'won't be any problem, I'm sure.'

'He's a wicked old flatterer, that man,' Gwen said and laughed after he'd gone. 'It was lucky you being able to come at such short notice, you know. With all the good weather we've had since Easter, the season's started early this year, and I'm rushed off my feet.'

'Well now I'm here, let me get started,' Lisa insisted, watching Gwen lift a series of scone-filled trays from the oven, before selecting a couple to slide onto a plate and put in front of her.

'You sit down, my dear, and drink that tea! Time enough to begin work later. I hope you're going to like it at the 'Mermaid.''

'I'm sure I will. I love old places like this. It's beautiful. When was it built?'

'Around the late sixteenth century, we think, but Matthew, my son, restored it completely a few years back.'

Her eyes brightened as she spoke, and Lisa could see the pride that glowed in them.

'Derelict, it was then. Hadn't been lived in for over a decade. Terrible state. It took a

3

couple of years of hard work, but Matthew needed something challenging around that time to distract his mind a little.'

There was a murmur of voices in the lounge.

'Excuse me for a second,' she said, hurrying out. 'That'll be the cream teas starting.'

Lisa was buttering her second scone when the kitchen door pushed open and Jamie hesitated, studying her with solemn blue eyes.

'Hello.' She smiled. 'I'm Lisa.'

'Can I have one of those too, please?' he asked, coming in eagerly. 'And jam. I'll get the pot. Gran makes it. With strawberries. We picked some the other day.' He was busily delving into a cupboard as he spoke, lifting out a jar, and carrying it carefully to the table. 'Why is your name Lisa?'

She laughed. 'I don't really know. I suppose my mother liked it.'

'I'm James really. Granpa's name was James. He's dead now. I can remember him, though. Gran's got a photograph in a silver frame. His face is like Daddy's only his hair is a bit worn out.' He spread the jam thickly, his eyes intent on the scone. 'I go to school. Real school, not play-school any more.'

'So there you are, chatter-box. Wearing out poor Lisa, is that it?' Gwen came back into the kitchen and began to load a tray. 'I thought you'd soon appear when you smelt my baking.'

'You must let me help with the teas,' Lisa pleaded. 'I'll never put all my training to good

4

use just sitting here eating your delicious scones, no matter how much I'd like to.'

'Well . . .' Gwen hesitated. 'If you're sure you're not too tired . . . I could do with a hand.'

'I do the serviettes, don't I, Gran?' Jamie interrupted firmly.

'Not with those sticky fingers, you don't, young man. We'll let Lisa do them this time. They're in that box. Four please, my dear. The rush is about to begin. Three more cars are coming down the hill and there's nowhere else for them to go.'

*   *   *

'That's where I sleep,' Jamie informed Lisa, having followed them up the stairs once the last teacup was washed, and two women from the village had arrived to prepare vegetables and start laying up the tables for dinner. 'And here's your room.'

He opened the door and Lisa saw a small room with a sloping ceiling painted white to match the walls. A pretty sea-blue duvet covered the low divan, with fitted cupboards above and on either side.

Through the narrow window she could see the cove where the tide was now high, waves pounding against the cliffs and sending up columns of spray that sparkled as they caught the slanting rays of evening sunshine.

'I hope it'll be all right for you,' Gwen said.

'We're all on this top floor, with the guest rooms down below.'

'Look, your shower's got seagulls on the curtain. Me'n Daddy chose them, didn't we, Gran? There's lots of different sorts of seagulls, you know. Joe tells me all about them.'

'Come on downstairs and let Lisa get unpacked. She won't want you chattering away nineteen to the dozen, young man.'

For a moment or two Lisa stood, gazing through the window, watching a group of fishermen preparing their boats to go out on the tide, wading into the water in long thigh-length boots, loading the big basket-like lobster-pots and nets. Above them gulls wheeled and dipped on silent grey-tipped wings, filling the air with raucous shrieks, waiting to follow.

It was all such a contrast from the town, with its streets of crumbling Victorian terraces, cars parked end to end, and a continuing hubbub of noise, where she'd been living before . . .

Before . . .

But she wasn't going to think about that, was she? She'd spent too many hours going over and over everything that had happened. It was finished now. In the past. To be forgotten.

She heaved the window upwards, leaning out to breathe in the soft air, tasting the salt on her lips from the wind-borne spray, hearing the sigh of waves as they tugged at the shore. The sun was quite low in the sky, sending long fingers across the flat surface of the sea beyond the cliffs, turning it to a deep coral-pink.

The view was all so gentle, so restful; difficult to imagine when a storm rose, sending mountainous waves to hurl themselves against the dark granite of those cliffs, turning everything into a thunderous tumult. Then it would become so very different. A terrifying place.

Once, she guessed from its name, there had been wreckers here. Smugglers even. This inn had been their meeting place. It was an ideal spot. A sheltered cove. Surounded by rocks. Miles from other villages. How simple to lure a ship to its doom.

The curtain suddenly blew inwards across her face, startling her, sending a shiver down her spine. I'm here to work, she told herself firmly, not let my imagination run riot.

*   *   *

As she took her place behind the tiny reception desk in the lounge later that evening, Lisa could see most of the resident guests were already clustered round the bar, chatting to each other and the barman. From the sound of their frequent laughter, it was obvious he had the knack of keeping them amused. She was curious to see more of him, but could only catch a glimpse of the top of a fiery head, as he

7

moved swiftly to and fro.

Then the outside door opened, and the first diners appeared, checking their bookings and handing her their coats, and for the rest of the evening she was kept busy answering the phone, or dealing with more people as they arrived to have a meal. Judging by the rapidly filled tables, she decided the 'Mermaid' was a very popular place to visit.

A few minutes before closing time, the door opened again while she was dealing with the last bill and someone paused at her desk.

'I'm afraid it's too late for a meal now, sir,' she said politely, without looking up from the change she was counting out.

The people crowding round her moved away and she realised that the man was making his way towards the dining-room.

'I said, we're about to close,' she announced firmly, stepping from behind the desk and hurrying after him.

He stopped, and slowly turned, regarding her with eyes that appeared intensely blue against the deep tan of his skin. The glint of mischief dancing in them sent a quiver of annoyance through her. It had been a long day. Tiredness was beginning to creep ominously through her. Her patience had reached a low ebb.

'Have you come to collect someone?' she asked sharply.

'No,' he replied, his gaze still holding hers,

'but I do intend to eat now I'm here.'

With a sigh, Lisa remembered her training at the college. One of the early lessons in hotel management had been how to deal with difficult or awkward customers. At least this man didn't appear to be drunk, although it wasn't always easy to tell, but seeing his height and build and the resolute way he was standing there . . .

She glanced through the archway. For the first time that evening, the young barman was out of sight.

Be positive. That's what they'd been told. A calm, but compelling tone was guaranteed to deter even the most determined person.

Somehow, she decided ruefully, practising on a friendly classmate had made it all seem far too simple.

She lifted her head, chin jutting purposefully.

'Matthew!' Gwen's delighted cry of welcome echoed through the room.

'Oh, Mother!' the man protested good-humouredly. 'Now you've spoilt everything! I was about to test this young lady's powers of persuasion. Come back in five minutes when I've found out more.'

'You wretch! It's Lisa's first day! She's spent hours travelling down from London, coped all evening, and now you have to appear and start teasing her like this.' She turned to Lisa who was standing, feeling both annoyed and

9

foolish. 'You've probably gathered this is my son. He descends on us from Plymouth every so often—usually when I least expect it—but his behaviour isn't always so thoughtless, I can assure you.'

'Good evening, Lisa.' Her fingers were gripped strongly and held. 'May I compliment you on your extreme vigilance.'

She glanced up at him suspiciously, not sure whether he was mocking her again, but his eyes met hers solemnly, reminding her of Jamie. That was the only resemblance between them, those intensely blue eyes. Matthew was as dark as his son was fair.

'Could I have my hand back?' The words were quietly spoken.

With a rush of colour, she realised she was still clinging to his fingers as she studied him, and instantly let go as if their touch burned.

'How's Jamie?' he enquired eagerly, turning back to his mother.

'Over the moon when he sees you,' Gwen replied, slipping her arm through his. 'How long are you here for?'

'Only tonight, I'm afraid. I want to look at an old school over near Marazion. There's a proposal to bulldoze it and use the ground for another car-park. It's a beautiful building, full of character and history, and I'd hate to see that happen.'

'So you want to buy it and restore it, I suppose? Oh, Matthew, it'll cost you a fortune,' she protested. 'Why not just put in a tender and have the car-park constructed yourself? That way you'd make an enormous profit.'

Matthew turned his head and gave Lisa a wry smile. 'My mother has no soul, you see.'

'But what would you do with a school, Matthew?' Gwen asked impatiently. 'You're not a teacher.'

'No, Mother,' he said lightly, 'but if everything works out as planned, I could even live in it.'

Lisa saw Gwen's face change to dismay.

'Live in it! Does that mean what I think it means, Matthew?'

'As I can so very rarely keep up with that butterfly brain of yours, my beloved parent, I honestly don't know,' he replied drily.

Gwen drew him towards the kitchen. 'Let's find you some food and talk while you eat.'

As they disappeared into the passageway, Lisa heard her continue indignantly, 'Surely you don't intend to settle down with that woman, do you?' Despite trying very hard, she couldn't catch his reply.

'Tired?' Andy, the fiery-haired barman, was slipping on a black leather jacket as he walked towards her.

She nodded, gazing with interest at his tall, rangy figure and freckled face. So this was the comedian behind the bar who'd been keeping everyone in fits of laughter all evening. He

11

looked about her own age. Nineteen. Twenty, maybe.

He gave her a friendly smile. 'You look shattered. Don't hang around any longer. Gwen locks up. She and Matthew will be nattering away for ages yet. See you tomorrow.' He tugged on a helmet and made for the door.

*   *   *

Through her bedroom window she could see the gaunt darkness of the cliffs silhouetted against the starlit sky. She'd forgotten stars. At home street-lights made it like day, casting an even yellow glow everywhere. Here there was a deep, smooth, inky blackness.

Far out to sea a light bobbed low over the water. A boat? She wondered. Did fishermen stay out all night? She could smell the salty wetness of seaweed and hear the soft slap of each wave as it met the shore. It was hypnotic, waiting for the next, and her eyelids began to feel heavy.

As soon as I slip under the coolness of the duvet, she decided, I'll be asleep instantly, but instead all the thoughts she wanted and needed so desperately to hide away, began to rush into her brain.

I'm not going to remember, she told herself firmly. Everything's over. In the past.

But her mind went on and on relentlessly,

12

refusing to let her forget.

Was it really only this morning she'd said goodbye to the other girls in the flat—all the girls except one—and caught the train? Already it seemed a lifetime away.

Would she ever see any of them again? Did she want to? They'd all been friends at the college. Close friends. Even she and Clare.

And they all knew what had happened. They always would. Did she want to be constantly reminded?

Ian's face filled her memory, and she felt a treacherous ache begin to burn her throat; tears stinging their way into her eyes.

I won't cry. I won't.

It wasn't Clare's fault.

It wasn't Ian's either. These things happen. Better now, than later, after we were married.

Her hand instinctively touched the empty space on her finger where once the diamond ring had been.

I'm not going to cry any more. I'm not, she told herself. But when she buried her head into the softness of the pillow, trying to forget, a torment of tears scalded her cheeks.

The sound of voices woke her. Sunshine was flooding through the gently blowing curtains, patterning the walls as she raised her head and pushed the thick tumbling hair from around her face. Climbing out of bed to pull back the curtain, she could see two figures, one tall, one small, crunching bare-legged over the shingle towards the sand.

Jamie kept up his usual stream of chatter and she could hear the deep notes of Matthew's reply, but not his words. Every so often the child would stoop to pick up something and eagerly show it to his father, before dropping it in the bright blue bucket Jamie carried.

The tide wasn't right out, leaving a wavering line of seaweed along the shore and she watched them step over it on to the firm, wet sand where the sea swirled round their ankles. Then Matthew tugged his blue and white striped T-shirt over his head, tousling his thick hair, and draped it round Jamie's shoulders, before plunging into the water and striking out with long, sure strokes.

She could see his dark head move swiftly across the surface and then he turned on to his back to wave, and Jamie waved back, the T-shirt drooping sideways to trail a sleeve.

'Not too far, Daddy,' she heard his urgent little voice call, and instantly Matthew began to make his way back. He gave the child a comforting hug, before taking his hand to climb the beach, the little boy trotting to keep pace beside him, the bucket slopping wildly.

Quickly Lisa drew away from the window, not wanting to be observed.

By the time she'd showered and dressed, Matthew was sitting in a well-kept ancient two-seater sports car on the cobbles outside the

14

open front door, while Jamie clung to the side of it with desperate fingers.

'Look, Jamie, I really must leave now,' he was saying urgently.

'But why can't I come with you?'

'You know it isn't safe in a car like this one, Jamie, when I can't strap you in, and Gran's far too busy to go with us.'

'Lisa can come then. Please, Daddy.' The child's eyes turned to her eagerly.

Matthew's gaze followed more slowly. 'Would you like to?' he said doubtfully.

For a moment she was lost in those deep, blue depths, then with a reluctant shake of her head she said, 'I'd love to, but I'm afraid I have work to do.'

'I'm sure we could get round that,' he answered. 'Sundays are never all that busy. As the guests are always out exploring the area, we don't do a Sunday lunch, only the evening meal, so there won't really be anything for you to do until then. Let's have a word with my mother. I'm sure she won't mind.' Decisively he swung his long legs out of the car and disappeared into the darkness of the lounge.

'If it means taking young chatter-box here, and giving me an hour or two of peace and quiet, then I shall be eternally grateful.' Gwen laughed, coming out to give Jamie's hair a tweak and then kiss the top of his nose to show she didn't mean it. 'Matthew's right. Sundays are never busy. Besides, it would be nice for

15

you to see some of the surrounding countryside. Cornwall's beautiful at this time of year. Any time of year, really. But then I'm biased, of course.'

*   *   *

'So you've been taking a course in hotel management,' Matthew observed, turning slightly, as the car sped along the twisting lanes, their high banks misted into a haze of pinks and blues where foxgloves, red campion, scabious and bluebells merged into a muted blur of soft colour.

Lisa nodded.

'And now what?'

'I need to get some practical experience for a year or two then, hopefully, start up on my own somewhere,' she replied.

'That's pretty ambitious for one so young.'

'I don't see why,' she retorted. 'There are plenty of opportunities in the hotel business, especially in a growing tourist area like this one. Age doesn't matter, although I must admit experience does. That's why I'm here. A small hotel like the 'Mermaid' gives a very good grounding in every aspect of the work.

'Besides, I'm not a child, you know. I'm nearly twenty-one.'

'And what about marriage? Isn't that included somewhere along the line? I'm sure there must be a patient young man waiting.'

'No,' she replied tautly, clenching her lower lip between her teeth, as she willed herself not to touch the empty place on her finger. 'Marriage is the last thing I have in mind.'

'Can we go to see the castle where Jack killed that giant in the well, Daddy?' Jamie asked, breaking into their conversation.

'St Michael's Mount isn't open on Sundays, Jamie,' Matthew replied, changing gear as they spun round another sharp bend, causing Lisa to clasp the little boy more closely on her lap, his hair blowing across her face like fine silk to hide the view.

'It does seem a pity to come all this way and not let you see it though, Lisa,' he mused, swinging the car onto the wide grass verge and pulling a crumpled National Trust handbook from under the dashboard, flicking through the pages quickly. 'There's a service in the church up there at eleven today. We could go to that if you'd like to. Could you sit still and be good for about an hour, Jamie, if we did?'

''Course I could,' Jamie retorted indignantly. 'Lots of hours.'

'It's nearly ten o'clock now, so we've plenty of time to get across. With any luck the tide will be out and we can use the causeway. Is that okay by you, Lisa?'

*   *   *

When they turned off the main road and down

17

through Marazion towards the sea, there was a mist hiding the water, then Lisa saw the outline of a stark rocky island appear through it, with the sharp upper edges of the castle lit by the sun, and gave a gasp of delight.

'It's just like a fairytale,' she breathed.

'Exactly like a fairytale,' Matthew agreed, 'although by the time you've climbed up there, you might not think quite the same way. The path's pretty rough, I'm afraid.'

They parked the car by the sea wall, and Matthew persuaded Jamie it was far too early for an icecream, then stepped down onto the sand to where a cobbled path led across to the lower tree-covered slopes of the island. On either side the sea rippled gently, and they skirted wide seaweed-filled puddles left in the hollows of the stones by the tide.

'We may have to come back by boat. The causeway's only uncovered for a few hours each day,' Matthew warned.

The mist was already beginning to drift away revealing more and more of the building on the rock-strewn summit, and passing through a collection of grey, stone houses by the tiny harbour, they began the steep climb upwards.

'That's the well, isn't it, Daddy?' Jamie shouted. 'By the edge of the path there. Jack-the-giant-killer dug it and then blew on his trumpet, didn't he? And the horrid old giant came leaping down to gobble him up and fell in and was drowned. It's not a very big well, is

18

it, Daddy?'

'That's because it's full of giant,' his father told him solemnly, keeping a very straight face. 'Come on, let Lisa and me have a hand each, or we'll never get you to the top.'

As they climbed higher, Lisa looked back to where the grey slate roofs and pink, yellow and white walls of the houses at Marazion glowed in the growing sunshine.

People probably imagine we're a family, she thought, watching the amused expressions of those listening to Jamie's excited conversation, and she felt the warmth of the small hand gripping hers.

Then they were below the high granite walls of the castle, crossing the battlements to the steps of the tiny chapel, and into its hushed peace. A shaft of sunshine patterned the pale uneven stone of the floor with jewel-bright colours as it filtered through the stained-glass windows, burnishing brass memorials to long-lost sons destined to rest elsewhere.

Jamie sat, for once silent, his wide eyes taking in every detail as he listened to the service.

'Maybe we could come back when the castle's open one day if you'd like that, Lisa,' Matthew suggested, when they stood later, leaning side by side against the harbour wall, watching the sea cream over grey-brown limpet-covered rocks far below where a cormorant dipped and dived.

'And me?' Jamie asked.

'How could we avoid it,' Matthew sighed, with a teasing tug at the little boy's upturned nose.

There was still time to walk back along the causeway, although Lisa kept a wary eye on the incoming tide that was already lapping hungrily at the smooth stones edging the path.

'You can just about make it when the water's waist high. I've done it a few times in my youth, but it was a bit hairy. I'm not sure I'd enjoy it so much now I'm aged.'

How old are you? Lisa wondered, studying his sun-tanned face curiously. Thirty? Thirty-five? It was hard to judge.

'Your waist is right above the top of my head,' Jamie observed, leaning sideways to measure, 'so what would happen to me?'

'You'd need a diving-suit, and that would probably keep you quiet for at least five minutes.'

Back in the car, they drove a couple of miles out of the village to the old school, a long, low building with mullion windows and topped by a small, white tower, still with its bell. Inside, damp stained the cobwebby whitewash of the rough walls and there was a musty smell that caught in Lisa's throat.

At the far end of the big main room desks were stacked, ink-stained and carved with wobbly letters, while on one side a rusty iron stove with a metal pipe leading up to the roof bulged with the remains of a coke fire.

'My school's nicer than this,' Jamie commented, wrinkling up his nose.

'I wonder what happened to all the children,' Lisa mused, running her finger over the rough initials on one of the desks. 'Some must be dead, I suppose, and others with children, or even grand-children and great-grand-children of their own now. And yet, their names will be etched here for always.'

'Or until someone chops the lot up for firewood,' Matthew said ruefully.

'You can't let that happen!'

'I don't intend to but, as land, it's a valuable site. There's a lot of competition.'

'There must be a better use for it than a car-park,' she said, rubbing a clear patch on the dust-grimed window to gaze out. Far beyond, over the pale slate-grey roofs of the village, she could see St. Michael's Mount rise majestically from the sea. It dominated the whole area.

'It's a lovely spot, isn't it? The sort of place to stay for ever.' Matthew spoke quietly, but she jumped at the sound of his voice, as if an echo had come to haunt her from far out of the past.

Stay for ever. A glimmer of an idea threaded through her mind.

'Would it convert easily?' she asked. 'To some form of sheltered accommodation maybe? Somewhere those who belonged to the village, and had once been to the school, might

21

like to retire to? It would be lovely to think of it continuing, not separated from all that history.'

Matthew stared at her thoughtfully, considering her words, his face slowly changing to eagerness. 'You're brilliant, Lisa! Quite brilliant. A proposal like that would stand a very good chance of being accepted by the Planning Committee too. Another car-park is only needed during the summer months, and there's plenty of space on the outskirts of the village. Come on, let's go and look at the rest. See what possibilities there are.'

He caught her hand and they toured through the other, smaller, rooms, Matthew's enthusiasm growing.

'It's such a practical solution.' He smiled. 'And so easy to interpret, without too much alteration to the existing building. Why ever didn't I think of it? Most of my ideas are a bit way out at times, I must admit, but I hate to see old properties, so full of character like this one, torn down. I just want to do anything I can to preserve them in some way that's acceptable, and useful, for today's society.'

Jamie came in through one of the doorways, his face covered in black smudges, cobwebs streaking his fair hair, eyes glowing. 'Can we come and live here too, Daddy, when we're old?'

*   *   *

22

They had their lunch in the garden of a pub in Marazion overlooking the bay, watching the tide creep across from either side to cover the causeway; seeing a few shrieking youngsters wading through, getting soaked as they did so.

Afterwards they strolled along the wide sweep of beach in search of treasure. Jamie had forgotten to bring his bucket, but Matthew found a plastic bag tucked away under the dashboard of the car and they filled that with a collection of 'treasures'.

Lisa sensed the combined warmth of Matthew and Jamie growing and extending to include her, welcoming her into their own closeness.

There was a harmony that seemed to unite them. Jamie was the common bond between her and Matthew, and she saw his relaxed smile turn towards her more and more as the child revelled in their company, his face one contented beam of happiness.

On the journey home Matthew started to sing the latest pop songs, and Lisa and Jamie joined in, making up the words they didn't know, causing drivers to turn and smile as they passed the noisy open car.

Back at the 'Mermaid', the three of them crowded in through the inn door, bubbling with laughter.

At first Lisa thought the lounge was empty, but as her eyes grew accustomed to its shade, she realised a woman was sitting in one of the deep armchairs, tapping the toe of an elegant high-heeled shoe on the polished wood of the floor.

Matthew stood quite still, not even his breathing was audible.

'Stella! What are you doing here?'

The woman rose to her feet and Lisa noted the sleek blonde hair, twisted into a severe pleat to reveal the clear-cut features of her beautiful face; then the coldness of her green eyes and thinning of her red lips as they tightened.

'More to the point, Matthew, what are you doing here?' Her voice held splinters of ice, and as she turned her head to stare at Lisa, the cat-like eyes became twice as cold.

'We've had a lovely day,' Jamie announced in protest, 'and now you've come to spoil it.'

Behind him, in the shadow of the doorway, Lisa silently echoed the words.

CHAPTER TWO

'Surely that child is old enough to have learned some manners by now?' Stella's voice was cutting.

Lisa quickly caught hold of Jamie's hand. 'Come on, we'll go and find Gran,' she said.

'Stella's horrid,' Jamie confided as they

24

hurried along the passageway. 'I wish I was Jack-the-giant-killer and could dig a big well and make her fall in.'

'That's not very kind, Jamie,' Lisa said severely, trying to hide a smile at the glower on his small face.

In the kitchen Gwen looked just as ferocious as she thumped a lump of dough onto the pastry board and began to roll it with short angry strokes.

'Would you like to feed these trimmings to the gulls, Jamie?' she suggested, handing him a plate and watching him step onto the patio before she turned to Lisa and burst out, 'Why, oh why do I let that woman get to me? As soon as she walks in through the door, I can feel my temper rise. Why can't I convince myself that if she's the one Matthew wants, then I should be glad?'

Lisa perched herself on the edge of the table and picked up a scrap of pastry, finding her fingers twist it into a thin noose, and hastily smoothed it out again. She'd only met Stella for a couple of minutes, but already she could sympathise with Gwen's opinion.

'Matthew will be off now. You wait and see. She'll invent some excuse or other. That woman can't bear him to be with us,' Gwen declared, savagely cutting out circles and spooning in jam. 'She's as jealous as a cat.'

She glared up at Lisa. 'Oh, I know I sound like a harridan of a mother-in-law and it's none

25

of my business, but Matthew makes me despair at times. First Rosalyn, now this one. You really would think he'd have learned by now. They're two of a kind. Beautiful, of course, but completely self-centred. It amazes me how he can be so blind.'

'They do say that men are always attracted to the same type of female,' Lisa reasoned.

'I really can't understand him,' Gwen went on, not listening. 'After his experience with Rosalyn, you'd imagine he would be doubly cautious. Scarcely more than a year his marriage lasted and only one good thing came out of that episode—Jamie—even though he does have his mother's colouring. Maybe he'll grow out of that as he gets older though.'

'You do sound bitter!'

'I am,' she said grimly. 'And I have reason to be. I've already seen one woman wreck my son's life. Now it appears I'm about to see another. He's following exactly the same path as before. I keep telling him. That's probably where I go wrong, but I just can't help myself. Matthew's as stubborn as a mule, determined to go his own way. Besides, there's Jamie to consider.'

'But you do want him to be with Matthew, don't you? After all, he is his father. They should be together.'

'With Matthew, yes. But with Stella . . .' Gwen's voice ended in a groan. 'All she's interested in is Matthew. She doesn't care a jot

26

about my grandson.'

'But surely Matthew must realise.'

'He does, I'm positive of that, and it's the main reason he's been holding back. Stella would have had him to the altar months ago.'

Gwen hadn't been wrong in her prediction. Only minutes later Matthew came through to the kitchen.

'Sorry, Mother. We'll have to be off. Stella's arranged a dinner-party and I'm needed to even up the numbers.

'We'll slip away without saying anything to Jamie,' he said quietly, looking out to where the little boy was scattering tiny scraps of pastry. 'He gets in such a state when I go.'

'Well, that's not surprising, is it?' Gwen retorted sharply. 'You're only ever here for five minutes at a time!'

'Thanks for coming over to Marazion, Lisa,' Matthew continued, ignoring his mother's anger and turning to her. 'I'll get to work on that suggestion of yours and submit some drawings. There's a Planning Committee meeting at the end of next week. Can you divert Jamie's attention while I nip off now?'

Lisa went out onto the patio. She didn't want to watch Matthew leave either. Not with Stella.

'Joe says it's going to rain,' Jamie informed her, licking the last crumbs from his fingers.

'Does he?' she said, glancing round. 'Where is this Joe then?'

Jamie's solemn eyes regarded her with faint surprise. 'He didn't want to get wet.'

There was a sudden roar of sound from the front of the building, and his face turned to dismay. 'Daddy's going!' he shrieked, rushing back indoors and Lisa caught up with him in the open doorway, tears of misery brimming his eyes as he watched the tail-lights wink on a bend before they disappeared up the hill.

'How about drawing a picture of Daddy's car to show him when he comes back?' Lisa suggested, trying to divert his attention.

'Too difficult,' came the gruff reply.

'But you're so good at drawing, Jamie,' she insisted. 'I saw your picture yesterday, with all those seagulls in it. A car would be much easier to do, you know. It doesn't keep flying away.'

He gave her a considering stare, wrinkling up his nose as he thought about it. 'I could draw Daddy too,' he said with growing enthusiasm.

'Borrow my red pen and this page from my notepad,' she said, lifting him onto the chair of her desk.

Children are such funny little creatures, she thought seconds later, watching the pen move busily over the paper. So easily distracted. And she wished it was as easy to forget her own misery.

*   *   *

'You must spend some time on the beach, Lisa,' Gwen suggested as the first week drew to a close. 'I'm not having you working non-stop. You're as pale as milk—not a good advert for a seaside hotel. A little suntan will do you the world of good. Do you swim?'

Lisa smiled. For one who never stopped working all day, Gwen was a fine one to lecture her. 'There was quite a good leisure centre near the college where I took my course. We . . .' Her voice died away. It was where she and Ian had spent most of their free time. He was training to be a sports instructor and fanatical about it.

Her mind was filled with the strong contours of his body; that straight firm neck with its short-cut curly brown hair; those cleanly defined features; seeing him poised high above her on the diving board.

She closed her eyes, hating the agony of her memories, and was aware of Gwen's shrewd gaze studying her. 'Yes, I do swim,' she said abruptly.

'Be careful of the currents then. They can be pretty treacherous round this coast. Many an expert swimmer has been swept out and not all of them come back again. I'd hate to lose you.' Gwen smiled reassuringly. 'Don't look so worried. The bay's quite safe, so long as you're careful. Look, it's always fairly slack from three until gone six o'clock, take time off then.

I can deal with any calls that come in at the desk.'

'But you work so hard already, Gwen,' Lisa protested.

'It stops me brooding,' the older woman answered quietly. 'You see, my husband Jim died a couple of years ago. I miss him so much at times. We had a perfect life together. I only wish it could have been longer. The trouble is, at the time, you take it all for granted. You don't realise, and it's only afterwards that you wish you'd said and done so many things, but it's too late then.'

'I'm sorry,' Lisa said softly, placing a hand over hers.

Gwen gave a rueful smile and quickly brushed her eyes. 'I'm being pathetic,' she said crossly. 'Some days it seems to catch me like this. Don't take any notice. Now, off you go while the sun's out. It's the first good day all week. Be quick though. Jamie will be home from school any second, and if he sees you, you'll have a companion.'

'I'd enjoy that. I'll wait.'

'Are you sure?' Gwen looked at her doubtfully. 'He can be rather persistent if he takes a liking to someone—and he certainly seems very smitten with you.'

'Good.' Lisa laughed. 'I've two young brothers of my own, and there's nothing I used to enjoy more than building sand-castles, but I haven't an excuse to do so any more.'

30

'We could take our tea,' Jamie suggested when she asked him to come.

'What shall we take?'

'Strawberry jam sandwiches. All squishy. And cake with currants in. I pick them out for the seagulls sometimes. Seagulls eat fish mainly, Joe says.'

They carried the basket of food, and what Jamie decided were useful things for the beach, down near the rocks.

'Put a big stone on the corners of the blanket, Lisa,' he instructed. 'Then it won't blow away. Daddy always does that. That's a good one by your foot.'

When everything was carefully arranged and the squishy sandwiches and cake eaten, he took her hand and led her down to the water's edge. 'Wash your sticky fingers, Lisa, then we can look for treasure. Joe says smugglers used to live here.'

His blue eyes were filled with excitement as he smiled up at her.

'In our inn, too. They were baddies and used to make boats get wrecked on the rocks and then steal all the people's gold and jewels. There's a cave round that bit,' he said, pointing to where tumbled granite bordered one side of the cove. 'Daddy and me paddled there when the sea was ever so far out one day. There was

31

a seal on the beach too. It wasn't very well, Daddy said. I think it died.'

Lisa slipped her arm round the wiry little body and gave him a hug. 'What sort of treasure are we looking for?' she asked, deciding it was time for a change of subject.

'Well, there's shells. Little twirly ones. And sometimes baby crabs and funny sorts of stones. And mermaid's hair. Look!' A finely patterned wisp of seaweed trailed wetly from his fingers.

'Just who is Joe?' Lisa asked curiously, bending down to pick up a tiny flecked shell and drop it into Jamie's waiting bucket. It was a name that seemed frequently to crop up in the little boy's words.

'Joe Trenoweth. He's my friend.'

'At school?'

He shook his head, scrabbling his fingers into the fine sand, and tugging out a hard white piece of cuttle fish.

'One of the fishermen?'

Jamie was carefully pressing his foot on the flat wet sand, leaving a perfect outline. 'No, he just lives here,' he said, waving his hand vaguely behind him.

'Where?' She'd never seen any of his friends on the beach, or at the inn with him. He seemed a very insular and lonely child to her.

'Look! There's Daddy's car!' Jamie was gone, racing across the sand and up the shingle, the bucket left standing while the

32

waves swirled round it. Lisa picked it up and slowly took it back to where the blanket fluttered in the breeze as Matthew strode across the shingle towards her, Jamie perched laughingly on his shoulders.

And Stella, Lisa wondered. Is she here too?

'A picnic? Anything left for me?' Matthew grinned, lowering his tall frame onto the blanket.

'There's just one biscuit, isn't there, Lisa?' Jamie told him. 'Only it fell in the sand so we didn't eat it.'

'We'll give it to the seagulls then, shall we?' Matthew suggested, and they watched as the huge birds swooped down to strut across the sand and greedily snatch up the morsels with long yellow thrusting beaks.

'Any news about the schoolhouse yet?' Lisa enquired. It was something that had been intriguing her all week.

Matthew adjusted his back more comfortably against the flat smoothness of the rock. 'I had a surveyor go over it on Tuesday and it's not in a bad state, considering. They closed it as a school about twenty years ago, so there's quite a bit of damp and general decay, but the main structure is in fairly reasonable condition. Far too good to be demolished in my opinion. So it certainly has possibilities. I'm going over to have another look at it this afternoon.'

His blue eyes had taken on a far-away look

and Lisa could sense his mind was already contemplating what he intended to do with the place.

It was a strong face, she decided, studying him thoughtfully. Not handsome, but good-looking even so. His forehead sloped steeply with thick dark brows and the clear blue of his gaze still startled her with its brilliance. His nose was a fraction too long and rather overshadowed his wide mouth, and she could tell from the thrust of his chin that he had a determined nature. But, all in all, it was a pleasant face. One you could grow to . . .

His eyes suddenly met hers again, and she glanced away in confusion, hoping he couldn't read her thoughts.

'I'm boring you,' he said. 'I get so carried away on my hobby-horse, I forget other people aren't interested in old buildings as well.'

'But I am,' she declared. 'They fascinate me.'

'Now you're just being polite.'

She laughed, watching Jamie burrow deeply into the sand with his spade, still searching for treasure. 'Why should I be polite?'

'Humouring me, maybe?' One eyebrow was raised in question.

'And why should you need to be humoured, Mr Pendeen?'

'Everyone round here seems to. I thought it must somehow have rubbed off on you, as well.'

She saw his jaw harden.

'I suppose, I did act like a bear with a sore head for a while.' His eyes met hers ruefully. 'People have long memories, you see.'

'Then don't forget I'm new and can only judge by my first impression of you,' she smiled.

'Oh dear! That damns me for ever!'

She'd forgotten that original meeting and a slight flush rose up her cheeks.

'Next time I promise I'll send a postcard so that my mother can prepare the fatted calf and you won't advance on me like a vengeful warrior.'

'I was exhausted,' she protested. 'It had been a pretty devastating sort of day.'

'And I was impossible,' he agreed.

'Well . . .'

'Still humouring me, Lisa?' he questioned gently, the clear blue of his eyes looking deep into hers.

'It's getting late,' she said hastily, rising to her feet and brushing dried sand from her legs. 'I must get back.'

'Must you?'

'Friday is a busy night. Surely you know that?'

'Don't worry. I shall be helping. You have yet to see me do my head-waiter stint. It's very impressive. Especially when I spill the soup in someone's satin-covered lap or pour wine all over the tablecloth.'

35

With a despairing shake of her head, not knowing whether to believe him or not, Lisa hurried back to the inn. As she towelled her hair dry after her shower, she couldn't prevent a glance out of the bedroom window to where he and Jamie were playing a game of cricket on the sand. The little boy really came to life when his father was there—and she wondered why he wasn't there more often. Then she recalled Gwen's words a few days earlier.

Stella's as jealous as a cat. She can't bear him to be with us.

And she hadn't forgotten the furious glare the elegant blonde had given when she saw them all crowd through the door together the previous Sunday.

Of course a man like Matthew Pendeen wouldn't be unattached. A young and obviously prosperous architect, he was extremely eligible—and attractive.

Seeing him laughing at Jamie down there on the beach, with his dark hair blowing in the wind, he was extremely attractive indeed.

So why were he and his wife divorced? Had it been over Stella? Was he, like Ian, easy prey for any woman who showed the slightest interest? Were all men the same? Never to be trusted?

She swung quickly away from the window and ran down the stairs.

*　　　*　　　*

36

Saturday was a busy day. There were guests departing from early in the morning, bills to make up and be paid, keys to check, taxis to arrange. Then, later in the day, the new arrivals began.

'Settled in, are you, m'dear?' The taxi-driver Tom's warm tones greeted her soon after she took her place behind the reception desk and she saw his weatherbeaten face smiling at her from the doorway.

'It seems as if I've been here for always,' she replied contentedly.

'That's Gwen for you,' he said. 'Makes anyone feel at home, she does.'

'Do I detect something more than praise in that remark?' Lisa enquired softly.

He gave her a sheepish grin. 'Is it plain for all to see then? She's a lovely woman, but she was very much in love with Jim.'

'And he's now dead,' Lisa reminded him gently.

'Some love never dies,' Tom said regretfully.

'No, but new love can grow beside it.'

'Do you think so?' He lifted his head sharply and looked back at her, his eyes full of eagerness. 'Would a man like me have any chance, do you think?'

'Why ever not?' She laughed. 'You're a poppet, Tom!'

'Encouraging admirers so early in the morning, Lisa?' Matthew's voice teased from

37

behind her.

'Ah, now don't you forget they say 'tis better to be an old man's darling, than a young man's slave, young Matthew.' Tom grinned, then Lisa saw his laughing expression change. 'I'm sorry lad. Don't take it wrong. I wasn't thinking . . .' But Matthew had swung furiously away and out of the room.

Lisa frowned. 'What was all that about?'

'Rosalyn, Matthew's wife, left him for a man in his fifties when Jamie was but a baby.'

*　　　*　　　*

Joe Trenoweth was growing to be a problem. Everything Jamie said or did seemed to be influenced by him. And yet, to Lisa, he was something of a puzzle.

'You live round this way, don't you, Andy?' Lisa asked the barman later that evening. 'So you must know someone called Joe Trenoweth.'

She was recounting an incident that had happened during the afternoon when Jamie had appeared, carefully spreading his latest drawing on the desk beside her to continue colouring, with a murmured, 'Joe says it's going to rain again.'

'Joe says?' she'd questioned, gazing out at the deserted patio, seeing it gradually darken as the first heavy spots began to fall. 'When did he say that?'

'Before I came indoors.'

'Just now?'

The child nodded, his concentration intent on the paper.

She looked at Andy with perplexed grey eyes. 'Jame's always talking about Joe Trenoweth as if he's just that moment been there, and yet I never see him. It worries me. He seems to be completely elusive. Who on earth is he?'

Andy's freckles crinkled into one blur as he laughed. 'This is Wreckers' Cove, Lisa. Surely you must know that Joe Trenoweth was their leader.'

She stared back at him, perplexed. 'But that was years ago, Andy,' she said.

'Of course.' He grinned, polishing a glass as he spoke.

'So how can he be Jamie's friend?'

'Oh, kids are like that, aren't they? Inventing pretend friends. I dare say young Jamie's heard the name and used it. After all, Joe was quite a character in his day and definitely famous in the area.'

'A wrecker,' Lisa mused thoughtfully. 'Not exactly the best kind of hero to have.'

'Wreckers have a bad name, I know, but in some ways it's uncalled for. Most were tinners from the mines that riddle the cliffs round this part of the coast. You must have noticed the old ruined engine-houses and solitary chimneys scattered everywhere. This was a thriving area for tin and copper a century or more ago. And tinners were so poorly paid and half-starving all the time that they regarded any wrecked vessel as fair plunder,' Andy told her.

'You see, some ships carried cargoes of food as well as goods, and after a bad storm the miners living round here would eat and drink well for several weeks. 'Twas only fair. The stuff would have been spoiled by the sea. At least it made up for the terrible conditions they suffered.'

'You seem to know a great deal about them,' Lisa smiled.

'My great-grandfather was a tinner and my grandfather has plenty of tales to tell. Ten there were in his family and the women and children all worked at the mine as well, but even then they had a job to keep fed and clothed. I'll take you up to the old workings over near St Agnes one afternoon, if you're interested.'

'I'd like that.'

So Joe Trenoweth had been a wrecker, had he? A man with a reputation for evil, whatever Andy might say. Lisa had heard of the terrible, murderous happenings that occurred years back in remote Cornish coves like this one, on dark nights when a vicious storm drove some poor ship for shelter.

Yet, Jamie made him sound so real, and the things Joe said were always true. Things that a child wouldn't even know. Couldn't possibly invent.

It was as if . . . Lisa felt a coldness prickle the nape of her neck.

As if Joe Trenoweth was there, close to the child, constantly, influencing everything he did.

CHAPTER THREE

Lisa woke early the following morning. The sea was flat calm, the tide coming in and Gwen had advised her that was the safest time to swim, so she slipped into her bikini, picked up a towel and ran down the stairs.

The cold shock of the water snatched her breath away, leaving her gasping, but once she dived under the first wave it wasn't so bad and she headed towards the rocks bordering the far side of the cove where the sun was already bright.

With a heave, she clambered up one of the smoother ones and perched herself on top, dangling her feet, letting the sunshine warm her while the long tangle of her hair blew lightly round her shoulders.

From the rock she had a completely different view of the cove. It reminded her of a jigsaw puzzle picture. Pretty Cornish harbours like this were always popular scenes.

The hill wound steeply away from it, with its

higgledy-piggledy collection of houses and cottages, their gardens ablaze with roses and paeonies. Below it lay the 'Mermaid', almost on the beach itself with the bay sweeping in a deep curve under the windows of the dining-room.

It looked further away than she'd imagined. It was probably an illusion created by the wide expanse of dark green water separating them.

Behind her, she could see into the next bay, which was merely a narrow cleft in the steep cliffs where dozens of sea-birds perched, waves lapping the sheer granite. Jamie's cave must be already hidden below their surface.

Looking back again, she saw two familiar figures walking down the shelving shingle from the inn and she could just pick out the bright blue of Jamie's swinging bucket as he trotted along beside Matthew. With a smile, she waved one hand.

The bucket waved in greeting.

More treasure-hunting, she thought, and decided to go back and help them.

The pull of the current caught her unexpectedly as she slid into the water, tugged her sideways towards the open sea. Panic stiffened her arms and made her legs go suddenly weak as she kicked hard with her feet against its growing force.

The distance from the shore was widening. In front of her was the rock she'd been sitting on only seconds before. By now it should have been yards behind.

If I panic, she told herself, it will make things worse, sap every ounce of my energy. Oh, why did I swim out so far? She asked herself.

And yet, it hadn't seemed such a long way from the safety of the beach. The rocks were a comfortable challenge, inviting her.

Gwen warned me about the currents too, she told herself, but even now the blue-green surface of the sea appeared calm, giving no hint of what danger lurked beneath its gently undulating surface.

Her limbs felt leaden. Useless. Fear was draining all her strength, leaving her too weak to propel herself forward any more.

She rolled on to her back, staring into the clear brightness of the sky, while a gull rose from the water, disturbed by her presence, and flapped heavily upwards into the blue with a protesting cry.

In a moment, she thought wearily, I must swim again. In a moment.

She closed her eyes against the searing brilliance of the heavens, letting her body rest.

A wave swirled over her head, choking her, terrifying her, and she fought her way to the surface, feeling the burn of it in her throat.

Something caught her chin, forcing her head back.

Her eyes turned desperately—and met Matthew's reassuring smile.

*   *   *

Jamie rushed to meet them as they reached the shore. 'Daddy said you were a mermaid, Lisa, when we saw you sitting on that rock with all your hair floating round you. Were you 'tending to be a mermaid?'

'Not now, Jamie,' Matthew urged, wrapping the towel round Lisa and beginning to rub her shaking limbs with ferocious hands before he swept her up and carried her towards the inn.

'Lisa's not a baby.' Jamie laughed.

'No,' she protested weakly through chattering teeth, letting her head sink into the comfort of his shoulder, feeling the light prickle of his chin brush her forehead. 'I'm not a baby, Matthew. I can walk.'

'When you act like a senseless child, then you get treated like one.' The anger in his voice startled her.

'I swam out a bit too far, that's all,' she said defensively, pulling the towel closer to her chin and shivering. 'I'd have been all right, once I'd rested a bit.'

'Obviously!' His tone was harsh. For a moment the piercing blue of his eyes burned into hers. 'Go and have a shower before you freeze,' he ordered tersely.

'There's no need to speak to me like that,' she fumed, still shaken by her fright. 'I'm not Jamie.'

44

'Just do as you're told, Lisa,' he replied wearily, lowering her gently to the ground. 'Or do you want me to carry you upstairs and put you under the shower as well?'

*   *   *

'Matthew's gone,' Gwen told her when she came down again.

Back to Plymouth—and Stella, Lisa thought miserably, visualising again the cold glare of her green eyes when they'd met the previous week. I've never seen such an unusual shade before, highlighted so expertly by a subtle hint of eye-shadow. Every inch of her is perfect. No wonder Matthew's attracted to her. Any man would be. She's every man's fantasy dream.

She looked down at her own cotton skirt and T-shirt, remembering the elegant white linen dress Stella had been wearing. On me, she decided dolefully, it would look like an overall.

'Does Stella work with Matthew?' she asked.

'Oh no. She runs her own travel firm,' Gwen replied. 'A very clever and ambitious lady is Stella. Started off working for one as a courier, then once she'd been there for a few months, took off and set up in competition. To be fair, she's made a great success of it. And she's always popping off to some exotic country or other, finding the right hotels and locations.

Quite a life.'

A rush of heat filled the kitchen as Gwen opened the oven door to remove some pasties.

'From her attitude to me, I get the impression that this hotel wouldn't even rate a mention in any of her guide books.'

'You really don't like her, do you?' Lisa asked.

'Do you?'

The question took her by surprise.

'Well . . . I don't know her yet,' she hedged.

'First impressions are sometimes the right ones,' Gwen declared.

In that case then, Lisa decided, I dislike her intensely. But obviously Matthew doesn't, she thought unhappily as she went out on to the patio where Jamie was kneeling on one of the chairs, resting his chin on the wall as he looked over.

'Joe says there's going to be a storm.'

The mysterious Joe again. A slight shiver of apprehension crept down her spine.

'Does he?' Lisa replied, scanning the deserted beach. 'Has he gone home?'

Jamie nodded. 'I 'spect so.'

'Where does Joe live?'

'Somewhere,' he said vaguely, scrambling down from the chair to tug at her hand. 'He's gone now. Let's find Daddy and play some cricket on the beach.'

'Daddy's had to go back to Plymouth,' Lisa said gently.

'But I didn't want him to,' Jamie wailed, his face crumpling. 'I wanted him to stay here with us.'

'But he has to work there, Jamie.'

'He could work here. He only does drawings like me.'

So why doesn't he live at the 'Mermaid'? Lisa wondered, and her mind was instantly filled with a slender, feline blonde.

The sound of the wind began to grow during the evening, waves thundering over the shore to pound against the sea wall, throwing up huge plumes of spray that hazed the windows of the dining-room. Lisa could hear it, even from her desk in the lounge.

'I don't fancy my ride back home tonight,' Andy groaned, hunching himself into his leather jacket and picking up his crash helmet from under the bar counter after the restaurant was closed.

'Is it far?' Lisa asked.

'Far enough in this weather.' He grinned.

'Why don't you buy a car?'

'A motor-bike's faster. Besides, it can travel over ground a car would find impossible. You'll see when I take you up to the old mine workings sometime.'

'Not tonight,' she said with a smile, listening to the sea.

'No,' he agreed. 'Definitely not tonight. One afternoon in the week maybe.'

'Take care, then.'

'I always do.'

*   *   *

The roar of the surf rolling into the cove kept her awake, and finally she climbed out of bed and pulled back the curtain, to scan the darkness. A three-quarter moon appeared briefly, then vanished as suddenly again, hidden behind the racing clouds, lighting for a moment the rock-encircled horseshoe curve of the bay. Enormous waves tore across, white-capped, to crash against the cliffs, sending their spray feet high.

An ideal night for wreckers, she thought, trying to imagine what it would have been like in the cove, nearly a century before. The moon gleamed for a moment on one gigantic rock jutting out beneath the stark straightness of the cliff. Was that where once a lantern had been placed, to lure some ship desperately seeking a haven from the storm!

And then, when it struck, swept on to jagged granite teeth hidden below the heaving surface of the sea, its sails rending in the force of the wind, its masts crashing down . . .

She could picture the bay, dotted with sinister dark figures, gathering along the windswept shore in silent shadowy groups. Waiting.

In the darkness a light bobbed and winked.

Lisa rubbed the misted window and peered

more closely. It wasn't her imagination. Somewhere out there a light glowed.

Wreckers' Cove.

But not in this day and age . . .

Silver faintly edged the clouds before the moon slid out once more, and she saw a figure silhouetted on top of the cliff.

Surely no one would be up there on a night like this?

A swirl of clouds scurried across the sky shielding the moonlight, and when they'd gone again, the clifftop was empty.

*   *   *

Since the weekend Lisa noticed that Tom Enys, the taxi-driver, had been coming in for an hour or so most evenings to sit at the bar, taking his time over a glass of cider. From the way his thinning hair was neatly brushed and his shirt obviously clean on, she guessed that their conversation about Gwen had had an effect. Everyone knew him and from the way they always stopped for a chat, she could tell he was a popular man, if somewhat quiet.

Gwen didn't fail to notice him either.

'Has Tom Enys taken to drink, Lisa?'

She laughed. 'Somehow I doubt it, Gwen. The 'Mermaid' certainly won't be making a profit out of his half of cider each night. No, I think it's the company that he's interested in, rather than the drink.'

'Company?'

'Oh, Gwen! Don't you realise that you're the one he comes to see?'

'Me?' A faint smile hovered round Gwen's lips and she pushed back a straying curl of grey hair. 'Don't be silly, Lisa. What on earth would a man see in a woman of my age?'

'You'd better ask Tom. Go and talk to him. He hasn't taken his eyes off you since you came into the lounge.'

'How can I, after what you've said? You've made me all of a fluster,' Gwen protested.

'And blushing suits you.' Lisa laughed. 'You look about twenty-five!'

'There's pasties in the oven waiting to come out,' the older woman said hastily. 'I must get back to the kitchen.' She fled across the room, giving Tom a swift smile as she passed.

In the bar mirror, Lisa could see the disappointment that flooded his mild grey eyes as he watched her go.

*   *   *

'When I close the bar after lunch, how about going to see these old mine workings over near St Agnes,' Andy suggested to her on Wednesday. 'It's going to be a lovely afternoon. The weather's always set fair for a while after a storm like we had at the weekend.'

'Great!' Lisa replied.

50

It was a beautiful July day, the sea a deep azure blue, so calm it was difficult to imagine its previous fury. Only the long leathery strands of seaweed with their rope-like roots, still heaped high up the piled shingle, gave any indication of the effect the storm had had.

The restaurant was filling with people, a few regular lunch-time bookings from retired locals, but mainly with holiday-makers touring the district, delighted to find Wreckers' Cove, and an inn like the 'Mermaid' with such an intriguing history.

Lisa guessed it was going to be a busy lunch hour so when the door opened for the umpteenth time, she carefully checked the table booking list before looking up, to meet Matthew's teasing blue eyes smiling down at her.

'I know,' he sighed, with a rueful shake of his head. 'You're going to tell me every table is full and I should have made a reservation. Maybe just a strawberry jam sandwich then?' he begged. 'I'll make it myself if you like.'

'Oh, I'm sure we can find a corner in the kitchen somewhere for you, sir,' Lisa observed gravely, trying not to let her mouth quiver with suppressed laughter at his woeful expression.

'Good,' he said, flopping down in one of the deep armchairs. 'And afterwards, if we can persuade my mother to let you finish your duties a bit early, I'd like to take you over to Porthcurno. They're doing a matinee

51

performance of "The Mikado" at the open-air theatre, and it's an experience that mustn't be missed on a glorious day like this.'

Lisa bit her lip.

'What's wrong?'

'I've arranged something for this afternoon,' she said regretfully, glancing across to the crowded bar where the top of Andy's red head glowed as he moved swiftly from one customer to another.

Matthew followed her gaze and she saw his mouth tighten. 'I see I also should have booked in advance for your company,' he said tersely.

'I'm sorry, but as I said . . .'

'You're already going out with Andy,' he finished for her. 'That's understandable. He's a nice young guy.'

'I really would have loved to come.'

'Would you?' The blueness of his eyes probed hers searchingly. 'Maybe another time then,' and he swung away towards the kitchen where she heard Gwen's welcoming cry.

Has he really come all the way from Plymouth just to take me to the theatre? she wondered, a flicker of delight pulsing through her. And where was Stella?

*   *   *

'Am I treading on Matthew's toes?' Andy asked as he locked the bar grille and caught

52

her elbow, guiding her towards the door. 'He glowered at me fiercely and muttered some comment about not letting the grass grow under my feet with regard to you, when I took him a drink.'

'He asked me to go to the Minack Theatre with him this afternoon.'

'You'd have enjoyed that. It's fantastic, especially on a day like this.' His grip tightened on her elbow. 'But you ditched him for me, is that it? No wonder he looked so fed up.'

'I don't break dates.'

'Only hearts.' Andy chuckled.

I don't do that either, Lisa thought hollowly, remembering Ian. Mine is the one that's broken.

Outside in the sunshine, Andy handed her a helmet. 'You'll need a helmet. Have you been on a motor-bike before?'

She shook her head, apprehensively regarding the gleaming black and chrome monster parked by the harbour wall.

'Don't look so scared! All you have to do is hang on to my waist and let yourself go with the bike. You'll be fine.'

As the machine roared into life, Lisa wasn't so sure he was right, but after they'd slowly climbed the hill, gradually increasing speed, she found herself swaying naturally with the motion as they leaned round every bend and twist in the lane, and by the time they met the broad main road she was beginning to enjoy the exhilaration.

In the distance she could see solitary high stone chimneys rising here and there from the yellow gorse-covered downland, and as they grew closer the ruins of an old engine-house, roofless, with tumbling stone walls.

Andy swung the bike away from the road on to a narrow track through scrubland and she could see the sea, like rumpled turquoise velvet, crinkle into the distance. As he slowed, weaving his way along a maze of criss-crossing paths, a lark rose high into the sky, its song floating back to them, and she tried to follow its flight but the brilliance of the sun dazzled her eyes.

'We'll leave the bike here. The path goes down too steeply to take it any further,' Andy said, holding it steady with one foot while she climbed off. 'Put your helmet on the handlebars. It should be safe enough.'

'You're very trusting.'

He shrugged his powerful shoulders under their black leather. 'There isn't any other choice. Come on.' His fingers curled round hers and tugged her towards the ruined buildings, where empty windows stared blankly from stark square walls.

'Watch where you walk. The heath's riddled with old shafts. They've capped most of them and marked those that are still open with posts, but you can still find one or two in unexpected places.'

'What happened to the mine? Isn't it used any more?' Lisa asked, looking round at the desolation.

'No,' Andy replied. 'Tin and copper were mined here from about the sixteenth century. There were a thousand or more miners working at one time. And their wives and children. Now there's nothing. The price of tin dropped in the early 1900s, and the lodes began to run out, so it stopped being a profitable venture.'

They were scrambling down a tiny path strewn by pieces of stone and rock, some glinting in the sunshine. Lisa picked one up.

'Is this tin?' she asked.

Andy shook his head. 'I doubt it. Probably a bit of quartz,' he said. 'Careful, it's slippery here.'

Lisa gripped his hand more tightly, leaning sideways when she saw the cliff fall sheerly to where waves thundered against its base several hundred feet below, and then, to her relief, her feet were on a smoother, wider path again.

'There was a lot of flooding in the deeper workings. Some run under the sea. So they needed a beam engine housed here to pump them out. This one's quite something, isn't it?'

They'd stopped in front of a tall narrow building, a few yards from the edge, its fat, tapering chimney rising high beside it, and Lisa peered curiously down through a rusty metal grid in the ground beneath one wall.

'Listen!' Andy picked up a stone and dropped it through the bars.

'I can't hear anything,' Lisa said after a minute or two.

Andy grinned. 'That shows you just how deep the shaft is,' and she felt a shudder quiver her spine.

'Imagine working all day down there,' he said. 'It was a rotten sort of life being a miner. Some of them had to walk miles across these cliffs, often in the dark and cold. Climb down several hundred feet of ladders to the shaft with a candle stuck to their hat for light. Work all day in the heat and wet, then climb back up and make the long walk home again. All for a mere pittance. It's no wonder they turned to smuggling and wrecking.'

'I should have thought they'd be too worn out,' Lisa mused.

Andy's thin face crinkled, sending his freckles into confusion. 'I reckon the thought of all that brandy and tobacco spurred them on. There wasn't much excitement to their lives.'

'Do you think it still happens round here?'

'Smuggling, you mean?' he said.

Lisa nodded, tugging a bit of thrift from a tuft growing beside the path and studying its pale pink flower. 'And wrecking.'

'Bit difficult, that. What with coastguards and helicopters and radar and such, a wreck can't escape unnoticed. But smuggling . . .' He

56

regarded her thoughtfully. 'They do say as it happens along the coast. There's many a tiny cove.'

'What about our cove?'

His eyes met hers in surprise. 'What makes you ask?'

Lisa shrugged. 'I thought I saw a light a couple of times.'

He frowned. 'Out to sea, or on the cliff?'

'Both.' She leaned against the sun-warmed wall, gazing at the endless expanse of sea, seeing far in the distance the low outline of a cargo boat, its bow washed by spray as it dipped and rose. 'I was probably imagining things.' She laughed. 'I'm as bad as Jamie.' Her face grew serious. 'But who would know? Porthrevy is miles from anywhere. It would be so easy to land stuff, or even people, at night. Who'd see them?'

'Well, you would for a start.' He chuckled, catching a curl of her hair before it blew into her eyes. 'Do you spend all your nights staring out of the window?'

His shoulder pressed into hers as he bent forward, tilting her face upwards, and she felt the brush of his lips before she could pull away.

'Is there someone else?' he said.

With an abrupt movement, she pushed the heavy, windswept tangle of hair from her face and turning back towards the path began to climb with long, swift strides.

'Lisa!' Andy's hand gripped her arm almost

fiercely. 'There is someone, isn't there?'

Once there was, she told herself, but now . . .

Ian had walked out of her life only weeks before. To Clare. Her fingers clenched round the place where his ring had been.

She looked into Andy's questioning brown eyes, eyes that reminded her so much of Ian's. They had the same eager pleading.

'I'm sorry,' she said regretfully, and began to lead the way up the stony track to the top of the cliff, her mind suddenly on Matthew, wondering whether he'd gone to Porthcurno after all.

It would have been beautiful, there in the sunshine. And if she had gone with him . . .

Then she remembered Stella, and compelled her imagination to cease its dreaming.

CHAPTER FOUR

'We'd better be getting back,' Lisa said.

'It's only half-three. There's no rush. How about a cream tea? There's a place over at Trevaunance Head.'

She pulled on the crash helmet as Andy kicked the motor-bike into life and began weaving along the half-hidden paths, before racing off down the road again, while she clung desperately to his waist, feeling her breath snatched away by the speed.

Finally the road trailed down a steep hill, then climbed again. Perched close to the edge of the cliffs, amid windswept lawns with leaning salt-burnt shrubs and trees, they found a small hotel looking down onto another pretty little beach.

Inside, they sat at a table by the window, watching the sea sweep in with long rolling breakers and a group of surf-riders crouched like sleek black frogs, boards poised ready, waiting for the perfect wave. When it came, they rose to their feet, curving in across the bay in one lithe movement, or vanished suddenly into the foam, legs and board upended.

'Do you go surfing?' Lisa asked, biting into a cream-topped scone, tasting the sweetness of the thickly-hidden jam.

Andy nodded. 'And wind-surfing too,' he said. 'Everyone does. Like to try some time? You can't live down here without being able to surf, you know.'

'I'm only staying for the summer months.'

'That's the time to learn then.' He paused, then asked, 'So what happens afterwards?'

'When I go home?' It was something she didn't want to think about. By the autumn Ian and Clare would be married. If she went back to the flat to join the other girls, she would never be able to avoid meeting them. And when she did? A pang of sadness tore through her.

'Is the thought of going home so dreadful? Did you commit some terrible crime or something? Is that why you've hidden yourself away down here?'

She gave a wistful smile. 'No. Just ... it doesn't matter. Don't let's talk about going home. It's not for months yet. I've scarcely arrived!'

'Then let's have another scone to celebrate.'

'I daren't!' She laughed. 'I must have put on pounds since I came, what with Gwen's cooking and lazing around on the beach.'

'You look all right to me.'

She watched a willowy sun-bronzed girl run down the beach to meet one of the wind-surfers, her blonde hair twisted into a knot on top of her head.

'What was Matthew's wife like, Andy? Did you know her?'

'Rosalyn?' He pulled a wry face. 'Almost the spitting image of his current girl-friend, Stella. They could have been sisters, they're so alike.'

So she was beautiful too, Lisa thought mournfully.

'And she left him?'

Andy nodded, lifting the teapot to refill his cup. 'I was still at school then so didn't really know much about her, except that all the guys around fancied her when Matthew brought her down to see the 'Mermaid'.'

He spooned in sugar and stirred the tea

slowly. 'From what everyone said, being tied to a baby, with a husband who spent his spare time renovating tumble-down buildings, wasn't her kind of living. And when some old man came along with plenty of money and a flash car, she was off like a shot. It really shattered Matthew. That I do remember.

'He used to come down to the cove every weekend, every evening, wet or fine, working on that place. No one dared go near him, he was that surly. Took him over two years to rebuild the old inn and around that time Gwen's husband died suddenly.'

'So that's why Gwen came to live here?' Lisa asked.

'Too many memories over in Helston for her, I suppose. She didn't want to stay, so Matthew suggested she took on the 'Mermaid'. Made a good job of it too.'

'And what about Stella?' she said, recalling those cold green eyes staring at the three of them on their laughing return from Marazion.

'Oh, she only appeared on the scene a few months back. Really something, isn't she?' He grinned. 'No wonder Matthew spends so much time over in Plymouth.'

Lisa gave a quick glance at her watch. 'We should be getting back now, Andy. Gwen has to do far too much as it is.'

'It's what she enjoys.'

'But she never gets away from the inn. She hasn't left the place ever since I arrived.

61

Doesn't she have any social life at all?'

'The 'Mermaid' is her life,' Andy replied.

'Then it shouldn't be. After all, she's not old, and she's still an attractive woman.'

'Not match-making, are you, Lisa?' he asked, eating the last morsel of scone.

'Yes,' she said firmly.

'So who've you got in mind then?'

'Tom Enys. They'd make an ideal couple.'

'Old Tom. But he's such a quiet old soul.'

'He's very smitten with her, you know. And besides, with a chatter-box like Gwen, he doesn't really need to say much, does he?'

'So that's why he's been haunting my bar each day,' Andy mused. 'I thought it was strange. Well now, what are you going to do?'

'Wait and see!'

*   *   *

As Andy's motor-bike shuddered to a halt on the cobbles outside the 'Mermaid' Lisa was surprised to see Matthew there with Jamie, wandering along the tide-line together. At the sound of the engine the little boy came scampering over the sand.

'Daddy's here!' he shouted eagerly, leaping into Lisa's arms and hugging her. 'He met me from school and we've been in the sea and I really did swim, didn't I, Daddy?'

Matthew caught up with him and swung the child onto his shoulders, bending in through the door with Lisa, while Andy wheeled his machine round to the back of the inn.

'Enjoy yourself?' he questioned.

'Yes,' she replied. 'We've been over to St Agnes.'

'And had a cream tea.' Matthew laughed, brushing her cheek with one finger. Didn't they give you a serviette?'

'Shouldn't you have gone back to Plymouth by now?' she countered, catching her breath at the feel of his touch on her skin.

'No,' he answered coolly. 'I've been doing your work at the reception desk so that you can have the evening off.'

Lisa stared back at him, puzzled.

'Well, you did say you'd like to go to the Minack Theatre, didn't you? I hope you weren't being polite again.'

'Do you mean . . .' she began.

'That I'm taking you to see the evening performance of "The Mikado"? Yes, I do,' he teased. 'But only if you'd like to come.'

'I've already been out all afternoon. Gwen . . .'

'My mother's perfectly happy about the arrangement, so don't worry. I told you I've been acting as receptionist. Maybe you'd better just check on what I've done though, and then if you've enough room after that cream tea, we'll eat a quick salad. You can get ready while I put Jamie to bed, then we'll be off. Oh, and bring a warm sweater. It can be pretty chilly up there on the cliffs at night.'

Lisa's mind was still whirling as she showered and slipped into cords and a jumper. What would Stella wear for such an occasion? she wondered, and angrily pushed the thought out of her head. Stella wasn't going, was she? At least she hoped not. Matthew hadn't mentioned her.

As she walked along the landing she heard Matthew's deep voice reading Jamie a story, and paused outside the bedroom door to listen.

'Are you going back to Plymouth after you and Lisa have been to the theatre, Daddy?'

'Not until tomorrow morning.'

'Will I see you before you go?'

'If you're awake very early, Jamie. I'll have to leave by seven o'clock. It's a long way to drive, you know.'

'I wish you could stay here for always and always.'

There was a long silence and then Lisa heard Matthew say very gently, 'Maybe one day, Jamie. Maybe one day, I will.'

*   *   *

'Do you mind the roof down, or will it ruin your hair-style?' Matthew asked, pulling the car door closed.

'I don't think my hair knows about style,' Lisa grimaced, pushing back the heavy strands.

64

'I'd much prefer the roof open. There's no point in having a sports car like this, if you don't.'

'Good. I hate being confined.'

As the car began to make its way up the hill away from the harbour, Lisa glanced sideways, seeing the wind lift and toss his thick dark hair over his broad forehead, his eyes concentrating on the winding road ahead, his hands firm on the wheel.

'So who are you comparing me with?' he asked, without turning his head.

She flushed.

'Come on then, who is he? There's been some heartbreaker in your life and it's not Andy, I know. You already had that fragile, broken look when you arrived. What happened?'

'I thought I was in love,' she said defensively. 'It's not unusual.'

'Not unusual at all,' he agreed lightly. 'But it all went wrong?'

She nodded.

'Go on,' he encouraged gently. 'You'll feel better if you talk about it. I do know what it's like. My wife walked out on me.'

She saw his knuckles whiten on the steering wheel as his body tensed.

'We were both at the same college,' she said abruptly. 'Ian was training to be a sports instructor and I was taking a course in hotel management. We spent all our time together.

Last Christmas we got engaged. I thought . . .'
Her voice died away as her throat tightened.

'You thought he loved you,' he said quietly.
'But he didn't, is that it?'

She swallowed hard, leaning her head back against the seat, the wind tossing her long tawny hair around her face as the car increased speed.

'He's marrying one of the girls I shared a flat with . . . they'd been meeting when I had classes in the evenings. Everyone knew, but me.'

'Better it happened now, Lisa, than later, after you were married. Besides, you're hardly more than a child. You'll meet someone else one day.'

'I'm not a child!' she protested indignantly. 'Don't be so patronising! I'll be twenty-one on Saturday.'

'Twenty-one! So old.'

Sensing mockery, she retorted hotly, 'Old enough to know that love hurts.'

'A broken heart hurts at any age, Lisa.' His voice held a note of sadness.

'I'm sorry,' she said quickly. 'I was forgetting about your wife. Did you love her very much?'

The car jerked forward as he thrust his foot down hard on the accelerator, and Lisa clutched the side.

'Rosalyn was very beautiful, and beauty is a great lure to any man, but love?' He pondered over the word. 'Sometimes I wonder. I, too,

66

was young. And when you're young, it's not easy to tell the difference between desire and love. That comes later. Knowing what true love means. Much later.'

'So what happened? Or would you prefer not to talk about it?'

'I made you confess and tell, didn't I? How can I refuse to do the same?'

'It is obligatory,' she replied, with a slight smile.

'As I said, Rosalyn was beautiful. But beauty is only skin deep, so the saying goes. Unfortunately I found it to be completely true. Beauty also can attract a man. For Rosalyn, many men. And she enjoyed that.'

Lisa saw his jaw tighten and an angry pulse throb in his cheek.

'It wasn't long after our marriage before I discovered she was merely a lovely face and body. Like an expensive painting, nothing more. No depth of feeling, not for me, not for Jamie. And that hurt more than anything. I thought, when we had a child, things would change. They didn't.'

The car halted at a crossroads, then continued on its way.

'For Rosalyn, Jamie and I weren't enough, we could never be enough to keep her contented. She needed constant assurance of her power to attract. I don't know why it worried her. She drew men like a wasp to honey. It didn't make for an ideal marriage.

67

'Eventually she found a man who had what she wanted even more than just adoration—money. So she left me—and Jamie. I could understand her leaving me, but not her own child. That was the worst part. Not that I ever want to lose him, but it made her seem so cold and unfeeling.'

He gave Lisa a bitter smile. 'In answer to your question, I doubt that my heart was broken as much as my pride. What kind of man must I be, that a wife leaves him, and their child?'

'She must be a very callous woman,' Lisa replied, seeing the unhappiness in his eyes.

'Perhaps I was the one at fault. How does one ever know?' he said, changing gear as they reached some gates leading into a field. 'This is where we park for the theatre.'

Carefully he edged the car through, avoiding people wandering across the grass towards the clifftop. 'Anyway, that was nearly five years ago.'

'And now there's Stella,' Lisa murmured softly.

'And now there's Stella,' he echoed.

CHAPTER FIVE

Lisa stood waiting while Matthew unloaded a couple of cushions and a plaid rug from the back of the car, then they walked along a grassy path to where a queue stretched away in front of them.

'If you don't arrive well in advance, there's no chance of getting a seat—and when I say seat, I'm being humorous, of course,' he told her. 'Wait until we get a bit nearer and then you'll see what I mean.'

Being so close to the cliff-edge, already, at half-past seven, the evening was beginning to grow chilly, and Lisa tugged her jumper over her head, pushing her arms into the sleeves.

'It's going to be colder than this later on,' Matthew warned, taking her hand as they went down the steep steps to where tiers of seats were cut into the rock, half-surrounding the open stage. Beyond was the sea, like a beautiful backdrop, while all around stark grey-brown granite rose from it dramatically, bordered by upward-reaching plumes of spray.

Lisa stared round, bewitched. It was unbelievable. A perfect theatre created by nature, and now enchanced by man into its present form.

'I thought you'd like it.' Matthew smiled, studying her reaction. 'It's even more spectacular when it gets dark, and tonight there's a full moon as well.'

They settled themselves on their cushions, with the rug folded beneath, and Lisa watched the tiers begin to fill, people slowly edging past, forcing them closer to each other, until the row was tightly packed.

And then the performance commenced with a flourish of brilliant silks and satins as the chorus of nobles stalked on, heads held arrogantly high. 'The Mikado' had begun.

When the interval came, the twilight had deepened leaving the stage brilliant with light, and beyond it the black velvet of the night sky, sprinkled with stars and an enormous rising moon.

With the darkness, it grew colder and Matthew pulled the rug from under them, tucking it round their legs, and swathing it up to their chins into a cocoon of warmth that made Lisa even more aware of his nearness.

From one pocket of his jacket, he produced a flask and poured hot coffee into its cups.

'Oh, bliss!' Lisa commented.

'I warned you it would be chilly. Do you want to go home now, before you really begin to freeze?'

'Heavens, no!' she protested. 'I'd hate to miss the rest. I don't even know what happens.'

'Is this the first time you've seen a Gilbert and Sullivan?' His dark brows twitched upwards in question.

She nodded, wrapping her fingers round the warmth of the cup and sipping the strong, hot liquid, savouring its rich taste.

'An unforgettable way to do so then.' He smiled.

Yes, she thought, gazing into the blue

depths of his eyes over the rim of the beaker. An unforgettable way to do so.

With the stage swirling in an array of colour, the final scene drew to a close, the clapping and cheers of the audience echoing away into the hush of the night. Then they began to gather up their cushions, rugs and blankets in a rush of enthusiastic conversation, as they slowly threaded their way up the steps towards the grassy track and the car park.

In the crush of people, Matthew's arm rested lightly round her waist, guiding her; but as they moved on along the moonlit path and the crowd thinned, it stayed there, tantalising Lisa with its strength and warmth.

When they reached the car, Matthew heaved up the folded roof, and she climbed inside. A button on Matthew's jacket caught the wool of her jumper as he settled into his seat and he bent his head sideways to disentangle it, his wind-ruffled hair brushing her cheek.

She could feel the warmth from his skin; breathe the faint spice of his aftershave, and for one heart-stopping second fought a desire to reach out and touch the firm line of his neck where the thick darkness of his hair peaked against his collar.

Desperately she drew away, hunching herself against the door, and saw him turn quickly.

'Careful,' he warned, 'I don't think it's

properly shut.' He leaned across to reach the catch. For a moment he paused, tugging at the door, and then the pressure of his body was gone again.

'Don't worry,' he assured her. 'You won't fall out as we swing round a corner, I promise.'

She heard the engine burst into sound and felt a wave of regret.

The magical evening was over.

Cautiously, Matthew edged the car into the line queueing for the gate and inched it through, following the gleam of tail-lights down the steep twists of the hill.

'How about making a detour and going home via St Ives?' he suggested. 'By night, from the top of the hill, it's quite something, all lit up for the tourists. Or are you tired? Would you rather go straight back to the 'Mermaid'?'

She gazed at him, seeing the strong thrust of his chin silhouetted by the faint glow from the dashboard. Slowly she shook her head in the darkness, a strand of her hair swinging out to rest on his shoulder, so that he raised one hand and gently detached it, twisting it round his finger into a curl before releasing it again.

'Was that a shake or a nod?' he said softly.

'I'm not tired,' she replied, and scarcely recognised the huskiness of her own voice.

'Good. Then we'll park down by the harbour and I'll introduce you to the delights of St Ives' nightlife!'

'Is there any?' she asked in surprise.

'No,' he replied and his laughter drifted lazily round her. 'But we can always pretend, can't we?'

Pretend.

That's what I'm doing. Pretending, she thought. Fooling myself.

But tonight I'm not going to think of Stella, or even Rosalyn.

Tonight I'm the one here, alone with Matthew.

From above, when Matthew slowed the car, the little town looked like a collection of jewels, multiplied and reflected back in the still waters of the harbour. A string of coloured lights garlanded the tiny quay, twinkling in the distance.

'By day, at this time of year, you can hardly find an inch of space to walk or park the car,' he told her, easing it carefully down the hill and through the narrow streets. 'But at this time of night, it's entirely different.'

'Can we really park here?' she asked anxiously, seeing the glint of the water as they reached the jetty.

'Don't worry so.' He laughed, smoothing a finger across her forehead. 'It'll give you wrinkles. Come on, we'll see if we can find something to eat. That prawn salad we had back at the 'Mermaid' seems a long while ago now, and at this hour at least we won't be besieged by marauding seagulls snatching food out of our hands.'

'Do they?'

'You bet! Anything they can grab. It's quite scaring at times.'

Chewing onion-rich hamburgers, clutched in paper serviettes, they strolled through a maze of winding passageways, too narrow to be called streets, gazing into shop windows.

A smell of frying and curry and coffee hung in the air, overwhelming the soft salt of the breeze.

'I wanted to show you the sketches I've made, before I dropped them in for the Planning Committee, but you'd already gone with Andy before I had a chance,' Matthew said, tossing his crumpled serviette into a bin.

'So what did you decide the school should be converted into?' Lisa asked, licking the last crumbs from her fingers.

'Why, sheltered accommodation, as you suggested. It was a fantastic idea. Those old classrooms will make suitable units and there's plenty of space. All we need now is to convince the Committee.'

'You must have worked fast.'

He wrinkled up his nose in a grimace, reminding her of Jamie. It was one of his son's favourite expressions.

'They're only very rough. Just ideas. Nothing positive—yet. But it should give them something to consider. Then, if I get the go-ahead, I can work on a more definite plan. I want to keep the building as near to the original as possible. Those mullioned windows are far too beautiful to lose.'

'And what about the bell-tower?'

'That too. It gives the whole place such character.'

As he spoke, the notes of a nearby church clock boomed out, echoing round the moonlit harbour.

'Midnight,' he murmured. 'The witching hour. I'd better take you home before we turn into pumpkins, or whatever.'

And, reluctantly, she turned back towards where the car was parked on the jetty.

*   *   *

A slight drizzle misted the cove when she looked out of her window next morning, hanging shroud-like over the cliffs, hiding them. A dank smell of seaweed filled the air, and even the gulls were silent.

Matthew had already gone when she went downstairs and Jamie sat at the kitchen table, the tears still wet on his cheeks.

'It gets worse every time Matthew leaves,' Gwen said quietly, watching her grandson with sad eyes as she sliced toast into triangles and slid them into three of the silver racks. 'Did you enjoy "The Mikado"? I didn't hear you come back.'

'It was a bit late,' Lisa admitted. 'We stopped in St Ives.'

'And ate hamburgers?' Gwen raised one questioning eyebrow, then laughed when Lisa nodded in amazement. 'I thought so! Whenever we went there when Matthew was a little boy, that was always his treat. He hasn't grown up.'

'Daddy buys me hamburgers too, when we go there,' Jamie piped up.

'Does he now? Then I shall have to have a word with your daddy, young man. No wonder you're turning into such a little dumpling,' Gwen replied, sending him into a fit of giggles as she prodded his tummy. 'Oh, and by the way, Lisa, Matthew said something about it being your birthday on Saturday. Your twenty-first. He thought we ought to do something special for it.'

'Oh no, please don't,' Lisa protested, surprised that he should remember. 'No one bothers about twenty-first birthdays any more. Besides I had a big party at home on my eighteenth.'

'Well, I've had my orders.' Gwen laughed. 'That's the same day as our monthly dinner-dance. Rather an old-fashioned idea I always feel, but it seems to have caught on. Anyway, Matthew said he'd be back for it, so I'd better do as I'm told.'

He'll be back! The words were still singing in Lisa's heart when she slipped behind the reception desk and began to work.

On Saturday, Lisa tried to pretend nothing out of the ordinary was going to happen. It was just another day. And yet a frisson of excitement made her pulse beat faster when she thought of the coming evening.

Jamie was the first, thumping on her bedroom door before she was even awake, then rushing in waving an enormous piece of folded paper.

'None of the shop cards were nice enough, so I drawed one myself, Lisa. It's a picture of you being a mermaid on that rock.'

She studied the widely smiling round head, thickly coloured with dark-brown streaks of long hair reaching down to a black winding tail that dipped into a sea of bright blue, where wobbly letters spelt out their message: *Happy Birthday from Jamie*. A string of huge Xs filled the rest of the page.

'It's beautiful, Jamie,' she said, giving him a kiss. 'The nicest card I've ever had. No one's ever painted one specially for me before.'

A smile of pleasure beamed across his small face. 'I made you a present too, all on my own. Well, Gran did some of it.'

He pushed a cardboard box covered with shells onto the bed covers. 'You can keep things in it. Treasure. It was my box, but I wanted you to have it, so I stuck all my shells on to make it prettier.'

'I shall keep my birthday cards in it, Jamie,' she said.

'Get dressed quickly now, 'cos the postman comes soon.'

Much to her embarrassment, Jamie insisted on arranging all her cards on the shelf behind the reception desk so that everyone could see them and she spent the rest of the day being congratulated by each arriving or departing guest in turn, even gathering a few more cards as time went on. But there wasn't one from Matthew.

And why should there be? she asked herself fiercely.

When, just before mid-day, as the rush for lunches began, a florist's van came down the steep hill and stopped on the cobbles outside, she was handed a ribbon-swathed bouquet of pale pink rosebuds and carnations. With trembling fingers she opened the attached envelope, her heart thudding with excitement, feeling quite sure . . .

Andy's name stood out blackly on the card, and she looked up to see his freckled face watching her through the crowd of people round the bar, and he blew her a kiss.

'Thanks,' she mouthed, trying to hide her disappointment.

The afternoon stretched emptily. All the new guests had arrived during the morning. The rain of the previous two days had cleared, leaving a sultry humidity, and after a swim she flopped on to her towel feeling limp and exhausted. There was a blurred look to the sky and the sea barely moved.

Jamie was indoors helping Gwen in the kitchen. Lisa had been banned from entering and wondered what they were doing so secretively, guessing that it was a birthday cake.

Every car that she heard descending the hill made her lift her head hopefully, by four o'clock she decided Matthew wasn't coming after all. Probably the lovely Stella had other ideas for his week-end, she decided.

As she climbed the stairs to shower and change out of her bikini ready for an evening behind the desk, she felt deflated and miserable. All the excitement of what she hoped would be a special day was gone. Oh, there'd been cards and presents, and everyone being kind. but somehow . . .

I'm thoroughly selfish and greedy . . . and horrid, she thought, using one of Jamie's favourite words. I'm working here at the 'Mermaid', in a job that I love, surrounded by people I like, and Andy sent me those beautiful flowers, and . . .

And Matthew didn't come.

Why should it matter so much?

So Matthew had taken her out one evening. It didn't mean anything. She'd given him an idea for that old school. It was his way of saying thank you.

He had Stella.
Beautiful, sophisticated Stella.

*   *   *

The air was even more hot and oppressive upstairs when she opened her bedroom door and went inside.

On her bed lay a long flat black box. She stood looking down at it, reading the name of a dress shop in Plymouth.

Plymouth.

Her breath came unevenly and her fingers shook as she slipped off the wide white ribbon tying it. Inside was a folded note.

For tonight's belle of the ball.

No signature. Nothing to indicate who had sent it.

She removed the crush of tissue paper.

A shimmer of silky sea-blue material slithered through her fingers as she lifted out the dress and held it in front of her, moving slowly to the long mirror on her wardrobe, her eyes filling with delight.

The colour glowed against her newly tanned skin, emphasising the tawny glints in her long brown hair.

In this I could almost be beautiful, she thought wistfully.

But when would there be an occasion to wear it?

She read the note again.

For tonight's belle of the ball.

Quickly she showered and then on slipped the dress, tying the narrow straps, feeling the coolness slide over her body to fall in a swirl of soft pleats round her slender hips as she stared critically at herself in the mirror.

How could he guess it would fit so perfectly?

With sweeping strokes she brushed her hair sleek and smooth, then twisted it into a thick coil on top of her head, revealing the long column of her neck and bronzed shoulders.

CHAPTER SIX

Matthew was sitting on one of the bar stools when she went down the stairs into the lounge, but it was Andy who gave the long, low whistle of approval; an approval that was echoed in Matthew's deep blue eyes when he turned to look at her.

'No reception desk for you tonight.' He smiled, rising to his feet and taking her arm. 'I've arranged for one of the other staff to do it.'

'You'll get me the sack!' she gasped.

'It is your birthday. And many happy returns of the day.'

'Thank you for the dress.'

'What makes you think it's from me?' he asked, regarding her with amusement in his eyes.

'Isn't it?' She'd been so sure.

He shook his head. 'That was my mother's idea. I merely found the right one.'

'Then I approve of your choice,' she said.

'And so do I, now I've seen you wearing it,' he answered softly, moving with her into the dining-room.

This was the first of the dinner-dances to be held since Lisa had arrived at the 'Mermaid' and the restaurant had been rearranged so that the centre was left free for dancing. At one end of the room a group played on keyboard, drums and guitars and, to her horror, they struck up 'Happy Birthday' with everyone enthusiastically joining in to sing the words, while Matthew led her over to a candle-lit corner table near the open french-windows, overlooking the patio and sea.

'This is all very embarrassing,' she hissed, wishing her cheeks wouldn't blaze so hotly.

'But why?' His eyes were full of amused laughter. 'You're a very special person tonight and we all want to tell you so. Any other woman would be delighted.'

Like Stella? she wondered.

'Some might,' she agreed grimly.

'Oh dear!' he groaned. 'Is that how you feel? And this is only the beginning.'

'What do you mean?' she retorted apprehensively. 'What else is there in store?'

He leaned across, his hand lightly closing

82

over hers. 'I'm sorry, Lisa. I shouldn't tease you,' he said. 'And I promise not to do so for the rest of the evening. I keep forgetting you're not a child like Jamie. After all, you're a grown-up now, aren't you?'

'I was before,' she retorted drily.

'But not looking quite like this,' he murmured softly, and poured the sparkling wine into her glass. 'Can you dance?'

'Of course I can!'

'Dance properly, not that disco stuff?'

'Yes I can dance properly, not that disco stuff.' She smiled. 'I am quite civilized, you know.'

Not that Ian had really enjoyed it. Not lively enough, he always complained.

'Good,' Matthew said, rising to his feet. 'Then you can show me how expert you are.'

The tiny square of floor was already crowded with dancers, leaving little room for two more, and Lisa found herself drawn closely to Matthew, the top of her head reaching his chin, his arm firmly encircling her, her body moulding to his as she began to follow the pattern of his steps.

'Not bad for a beginner,' he teased, and she felt his mouth smile against her cheek, then he led her back to their table as the waiter appeared with the cool slices of melon and orange they'd ordered.

The meal was delicious. Somehow, tonight everything tasted surprisingly different to Lisa.

She ate at the inn every day, but not in these surroundings. Despite the crowded room their candlelit table seemed an island set apart from the rest.

Eagerly, she studied the menu but Matthew wouldn't let her order a sweet.

'Wait,' he said firmly. 'And see.'

The lights were lowered. A sudden hush fell on the room. And then, with a rattle of wheels, a snowy-clothed trolley was wheeled from the kitchen, candle flames quivering in the rush of air as it moved across the room to their table. For a moment, in the glow of their wavering circle of light, she and Matthew appeared to be the only people there, before she blew out the flames, leaving a shadowy darkness.

The size of the cake amazed her. How had Gwen concealed such a superb confection? Crisp, golden-tinted meringue covered a centre of ice-cream, thick with strawberries and clotted-cream. The taste was out of this world.

'Those aren't tears, are they?' Matthew gently tilted her chin.

'I've never had a birthday like this before. Everyone's been so kind, and you . . .' Her voice faltered.

'It's a pity Jamie couldn't join in. He'd have enjoyed all this.' His fingers touched hers lightly. 'Not many would bother with a lonely little boy, like you do. Thank you, Lisa.'

'Jamie's a delight,' she declared. 'An

adorable child.' She looked up at him through tear-wet lashes. 'It's a pity you can't be with him more often. He misses you so much.

'Do you have to live in Plymouth?'

'It's where I work,' he replied stiffly.

'Jamie thinks you could "do your drawing" here just as well.'

'Then Jamie's wrong,' he said abruptly. 'Now, shall we dance again while we wait for coffee?'

Everyone else seemed to have the same idea and the space was so confined that all they could do was sway from side to side without moving from one spot, and with a sigh of impatience Matthew drew her towards the open french-windows and onto the patio, where the music drifted out on the heavy night air.

Even there it was hot and sultry. Lisa could feel the burn of Matthew's cheek against her skin, and closed her eyes, content to stay there for ever.

A sudden jag of brightness made her open them again and the whole sky shivered with light, then came the low ominous rumble of thunder, and she gripped Matthew's hand more tightly.

'You're not afraid of storms, are you?' The words trembled through the mist of her hair.

She nodded, and felt his lips brush her forehead with the movement, then pause, and begin to feather their way softly down the line of her cheek, towards her mouth. Instinctively she turned, raising her face, letting his lips possess hers, lightly at first, then more fiercely as his hand slid up her neck to tangle in her hair, loosening the pins that held it high on her head.

When the first drops of rain began to fall, still they clung together, not even noticing, until Matthew slowly released her, the blue of his eyes so intense that she could almost feel their fire.

'You're getting drenched.' His voice was husky, his arm slipping round her shoulders to guide her across the patio and in through the door of the lounge. Quickly she twisted her hair back into its restraining knot, her confused eyes meeting Andy's as he stood staring at them across the room from the bar.

'I'll get you a drink. A liqueur?' Matthew was moving away and she wanted to catch at his sleeve, to keep him there beside her, never to go.

Not trusting her voice, she nodded.

The spell was broken.

'I'd almost forgotten your birthday present,' he said on his return. 'Wait here, while I fetch it.'

She took the slender glass from his hand, raising it quickly to her lips, trying to cool the heat of the kiss that still flamed there, not wanting to look into his eyes, fearing what her own would reveal.

Andy watched him climb the stairs. 'I don't stand a chance, do I, against a man like that?' he said regretfully.

'What do you mean?'

'Oh, come on, Lisa. It's pretty obvious what's happening. A candlelit dinner for two. You, in a dress like that. And then, out there on the patio.' He silenced her protest with a frown. 'Don't try to tell me nothing happened. I saw how you looked when you came in through that door.'

'You've got it all wrong, Andy,' she protested hotly. 'The dinner was just a way to say thank you for being kind to Jamie, and the dress was a present from Gwen. We were only dancing out there . . . because the floor was so crowded . . . that's all there was to it.'

But she knew the scarlet burning in her cheeks made her words a lie and that from the expression in his eyes, Andy wasn't fooled at all.

'That's not the impression I had when you both came indoors, Lisa,' he replied.

'But it's true!'

'Is it?' he enquired softly.

'Happy birthday!' Matthew was back, holding a small gold-wrapped packet.

Avoiding Andy's gaze, she slowly undid it.

A delicate watercolour of St Michael's Mount lay there in the crumpled folds of paper, just as she remembered it, the castle rising high above the slight mist; a fairytale setting, elusive and mysterious with trees covering the island, green and thick behind the grey stone houses gathered by the harbour; the sea below a gentle blue bordering the pale stone of the causeway.

'I painted it a while back, but I thought it might appeal to you.'

'It's beautiful.' Her eyes glowed with pleasure as she smiled up at him. 'I didn't realise you painted as well. Thank you, Matthew.'

'Thank *you*, Lisa,' he replied, and she was instantly aware of the expression on Andy's face as he looked at her from behind Matthew's back.

Then, with a muffled sob, a tearful little figure came trailing down the stairs, clutching a bedraggled teddy. Lisa quickly ran across to comfort Jamie.

'The dark's making a horrid noise and I don't like it,' he wailed, burying his head against her shoulder.

'It's only thunder, Jamie,' she soothed.

'I don't like it, Lisa. I keep thinking all the roof's going to fall on top of me.'

'Well, don't worry, Jamie, it's not going to,' Matthew replied sitting on his heels beside the child. 'The 'Mermaid' has been here through dozens of storms, far worse than this one, and it's still as sturdy as ever.'

'But that's because you builded it up again, Daddy. It was all fallen down when you found it. Joe said so.'

'Joe?' Matthew raised one questioning eyebrow at Lisa.

'Joe Trenoweth,' she explained. 'Jamie's friend.'

'But ...' Matthew began, and Lisa interrupted him swiftly.

'He's only pretend, isn't he, Jamie?'

'He's not pretend.' Jamie frowned. 'He's my friend.'

'Okay, Jamie, let's go up to bed again, shall we?'

Matthew lifted the tired little boy into his arms and began to climb the stairs.

'Lisa too,' Jamie insisted, reaching out to her.

'Lisa too, and if you ask her nicely, maybe she'll read you a story and then you can go to sleep.'

'Will you, Lisa?' the child asked drowsily.

'Of course I will.' She smiled.

*   *   *

Afterwards, when they were back in the lounge, with Jamie asleep again, and all the diners gone, Matthew asked her, 'What's all this about Joe Trenoweth? You know who he was, don't you?'

'A wrecker,' Lisa answered. 'And he lived round this way.'

'So what's Jamie going on about?'

'He's invented an imaginary friend, that's all. Lonely children often do, you know. And obviously that name appealed.' She frowned slightly. 'Only he does seem to make him very real. He frequently tells me something that Joe has said, and nearly always whatever it is happens soon after. Joe seems very good at predicting storms.'

'He probably would be!' Matthew smiled. 'They were an essential part of his way of life.' Distractedly he pushed his fingers through his thick hair, rumpling its smooth darkness. 'I don't like it though. It's all very well for a child to have an imagination, but not like this.'

Lisa nodded. 'To be honest, I find it a bit creepy too, especially when those strange lights appear at night.'

Matthew looked at her sharply. 'What do you mean?'

'I've seen them several times recently. Out to sea, sort of winking, and sometimes up on the cliff.'

'Now who has the vivid imagination?' Matthew laughed. 'There's a perfectly simple explanation for those. Every boat carries a light at night.'

'Not winking,' she persisted.

'Distance makes things appear to wink. Think of the stars. That's why they twinkle.'

'And what about the lights over on the clifftop?'

'Someone out for a walk probably,' he

suggested.

'In the middle of the night?' she scorned.

'How about a ghostly miner wending his way home?' he teased. 'That's the route some of them took in those days.'

'Don't say that, Matthew!'

'You *are* scared, aren't you?' he said, leaning forward, his face concerned.

'Jamie is rather convincing about Joe Trenoweth.'

'Joe's quite dead, I can assure you. Hanged from a gibbet on top of the hill for all his wicked deeds.'

'Matthew!'

'Don't get so upset! Anyway I'll check up on his history when I get back from Greece.'

'Greece?' The word echoed hollowly in her ears.

'Yes. Stella runs her own travel business and she's found some remote little Greek island she wants my opinion on, before she starts sending scores of tourists there.'

'But what about the Planning Committee meeting and the old school?'

He smiled lazily at her. 'Didn't I tell you? I'm sorry, I meant to, but with all the excitement of your birthday . . . They snapped up the idea. I'm going over to Marazion to have another look at the place in the morning. Like to come again?'

Stretching out his long legs, he leaned back into the depths of the sofa and continued, 'A

91

remote island will be the ideal place to work on some sketches. That's one of my reasons for going. In Plymouth everyone else would get in the way. With nothing but peace and quiet, I'll have plenty of time to get my ideas down on paper.'

One of the reasons. But what are the others? Lisa wondered dejectedly.

'I had a phone call from the chairman of the Committee after the meeting,' he went on, 'so stopped off to see him on my way down here. That's why I was so late arriving. I'd intended to be here much sooner. And I had to pack a few things as well. Not that you need much in a place like that. A pair of swimming trunks should do.'

Every word he spoke hammered into Lisa. She could picture Stella in a brief scrap of a bikini, stretched out on some golden, sun-drenched beach. A remote little island, Matthew had said. She doubted he would get much work done, if Stella had her way.

'Have you enjoyed your birthday?'

'Yes,' she said slowly.

Until now, she wanted to add.

He smiled, reaching out to tuck back a strand of her hair that had tumbled from the half-pinned coil on her head.

'Jamie's very fond of you, you know.'

Only Jamie, she thought wistfully.

His fingers were still lost in her hair, and she saw the clear blue of his eyes darken to ink when she turned her head; then his face was moving closer.

The sound of a car engine flooded the air. Headlights swept across the windows, illuminating the pale walls of the room. A murmur of voices came from outside as a car door closed softly, and the engine note rose again to fade into the distance.

Gwen came in from the porch, hesitating when she saw them.

'Oh,' she faltered, looking confused. 'I thought everyone would be asleep by now.'

'And where have you been, Mother?' Matthew grinned wickedly, rising from the sofa to cross the room and meet her.

Gwen drew herself up to her full height and glowered at her son.

'I am old enough to go out without asking permission, you know.'

'Of course you are, Mother, but where have you been, and more importantly, with whom?'

'Tom and I went out for coffee.' A sparkle brightened her eyes as she spoke.

'At this time of night?' Matthew's lips twitched with humour.

'You're not the only one to enjoy the nightlife of St Ives, you know.' She chuckled.

'Oh, Mother, not hamburgers as well! You'll never sleep.'

'No.' She laughed. 'Just coffee.'

'You could have had some here,' he suggested slyly.

'We could,' she replied loftily, 'but chose not to. After all, there are people around who might gossip. And others,' she went on, staring purposefully at him, 'who would tease. So if you've finished your inquisition, I'm feeling rather tired and I've a busy day tomorrow.'

'Good night, Mother,' he replied solemnly. 'Oh, and by the way, your lipstick's smudged!'

With a furious glare at him, Gwen rubbed hastily at her mouth and hurried up the stairs.

'Well, well,' he remembered, after she'd gone. 'Would you believe it?'

'Yes,' Lisa replied. 'I suggested it to Tom.'

She picked up the little painting from where it lay on one of the coffee tables. 'And now, I'll follow Gwen's example and go to bed too.'

*   *   *

Her fingers smoothed the silky fabric as she slid the dress on to its hanger then studied the note. It wasn't Gwen's writing. She knew that quite well. Was it Matthew's, though?

Was the dress really his own idea, despite what he said? The words were so like him.

An unpleasant thought crept into her brain as she looked at the box again. A small, exclusive shop in Plymouth. Just the sort of place Stella would patronise. Surely he hadn't asked her to choose something suitable? No, Stella wouldn't have chosen a dress like this one for her, she felt sure.

So was it Matthew?

She could still feel the burn of his lips on hers when they were dancing out there on the patio; the touch of his fingers tangling into her hair.

But he was going away. To a remote Greek island—with Stella.

Stella. The cool elegant blonde who reminded everyone so much of his wife, Rosalyn.

And Matthew had loved Rosalyn, hadn't he? Wasn't that what he'd been trying to tell her when they travelled to Porthcurno the other day?

He must have loved her, or he wouldn't have chosen another woman in her image.

She looked in the mirror at her own face, surrounded by its untidy mist of tawny hair.

No one would ever call her beautiful.

Even that lovely dress couldn't change her into a tall, sophisticated, mature blonde.

Through the open window she could hear the sea, still roaring up the beach after the sudden storm. She went across the room to pull it closed. The sultry heat had gone now, leaving a clammy chill in the air.

In the distance a light winked. Once. Twice. Three times.

And from the clifftop came a gleam as if in answer.

CHAPTER SEVEN

The light on the cliff blinked again. Lisa was certain it was signalling. It was too much of a coincidence.

And out to sea came the response. Once. Twice. Three times.

It had to be a signal.

Should she go and tell Matthew? He probably wasn't asleep yet. She hesitated. If she did and the light didn't appear again, then he'd only laugh and tease her. He'd say it was more of her wild imagination, like Jamie.

Matthew seemed to spend all his time comparing her with Jamie, as if she were a child. Her finger touched her cheek, tracing the path his lips had made before they reached her mouth. He certainly hadn't thought her a child then. No man had kissed her like that before. Not even Ian.

She realised that she hadn't thought of Ian for days now. He hadn't sent a card for her birthday. But then, why should he? He and Clare would be married in a month or so.

With an effort, she tried to remember the square outline of his face; his brown eyes—or were they blue? The clear outstanding shade of Matthew's eyes filled her mind, intensely blue. But Ian's . . .

And his hair. Fair. Almost golden. Or was it darker, more of a tawny brown? Could I really have forgotten so soon? she asked herself.

Only months ago I thought my heart was broken for ever, but now . . . Is it to be broken again?

Why do I always fall in love with the wrong man?

It's all so complicated, she told herself. I was in love with Ian, then he fell in love with Clare. And now it's Matthew who fills my every waking moment.

And Matthew loves Stella, she reminded herself.

A rueful smile twisted her lips.

Was that what was meant by an eternal triangle?

She stared out into the blackness of the night, watching and waiting. The minutes ticked away. She yawned.

No more lights gleamed.

A fishing boat, Matthew said, carrying lights. He was probably right. She was imagining things.

Sleepily, she pulled back the covers and climbed into bed.

*   *   *

Jamie didn't go with them to Marazion this time. Tom Enys had suggested to Gwen that they take him over to the Aero Park near Helston and as Sunday was always a quiet day for the 'Mermaid', she agreed.

As Matthew drove along Lisa searched eagerly for the first breathtaking sight of the island, rising from the sea, with the castle perched on its summit. Once again it didn't disappoint her.

'Still like a fairytale?' Matthew asked softly.

She nodded contentedly, remembering the peace of the little church, its floor dappled with jewel colours by sunshine through the beautiful stained glass windows at one end.

Centuries of prayer seemed to hang in the air, quivering in every sunbeam. And she recalled how Matthew had sat beside her, his head bent for a moment, his eyes closed.

'Here's the school.' Matthew's voice broke into her thoughts as the car stopped.

She could imagine it as once it had been with children there, its playground a babble of shrieks and laughter. The year had changed all that. Now weeds grew up through the black crumbling tarmac and a thin sapling had rooted itself in one of the gutters.

The view from its windows was the same as it had always been, though. Nothing could change that, not even time, she thought, gazing at the outline of the castle and the wide sweep of Mounts Bay.

Those square walls had guided sailing ships into the safety of its tiny harbour, seen blood-drenched battles rage along its shores, and were still towering there, their rock as stark and bleak as it always had been.

Matthew went from room to room, making quick sketches, his expression intent, creating a future for this derelict school.

How could anyone want to tear it down and make a car park on the site, she wondered, glancing up at the domed little tower with its silent bell and the creamy stone of the mullioned windows, some panes shattered, letting in the damp and chill.

But Matthew would change all that. Inside the shell of this lovely building, homes would grow; voices and laughter would fill the air. The place would come alive again. Matthew would make it happen with his love for old buildings and firm resolution not to let them vanish, losing all their history and beauty.

From across the room where scratched and ink-stained desks were piled against one wall, she watched him turn, his eyes blazing with enthusiasm, and then he smiled.

It was a smile that drew her towards him, making her forget everything and everyone that existed. Only that he was there. That she was there. Nothing else mattered.

Somewhere in the distance a church clock chimed.

'Time to get back,' he said, almost reluctantly.

And she remembered that, this time tomorrow, he and Stella would be together, on a Greek island.

Rain pattered down. Lisa sat at the reception desk gazing through the window, trying to decide where the sea ended and the sky began. Both were the same dull leaden grey. It was a dreary Monday.

Guests sat in the lounge, reading newspapers, looking up every now and then in case the weather had changed.

Jamie marched in. Today he was on holiday from school while part of the roof was retiled. From the woebegone expression on his face she guessed he was still missing Matthew.

She moved one of the bar stools to behind her desk, and lifted him onto it, suggesting he draw a picture.

'What of?' he pouted crossly.

'Oh, anything you like,' she said, sorting through the morning's post to organise new bookings.

'You tell me something,' he demanded.

'How about a picture of . . .' She wracked her brain frantically. 'Joe,' she said.

'Easy-peasy.' Jamie smiled, picking up a felt-tipped pen.

She hadn't expected a boat, and yet there was a black stick-like creature standing up in one, with a wide expanse of blue sea all round and some dark brown scribble in the background.

'What's that meant to be?' she asked

100

curiously.

'I haven't finished yet,' Jamie told her sternly. 'That's the cliffs and that's the mermaid.' With a final flourish, he produced a bright yellow ball of colour.

'It doesn't look like a mermaid to me,' Lisa said. 'You did a much nicer one on my birthday card.'

'It's not the same sort of mermaid.'

'What do you mean? Mermaids are beautiful ladies with long fishy tails, aren't they?'

'Not sometimes. Our mermaid wasn't.'

'Of course she was, Jamie. Every mermaid is the same.'

The little boy glowered at her. 'Joe's told me all about our mermaid. It was a lantern.'

'A lantern?' Lisa laughed. 'Well, Joe's got it all wrong.'

'He hasn't,' Jamie insisted, his voice rising. 'Joe knows. He put it out.'

'Put what out?' Lisa asked, mystified.

'The lantern, silly. That's when his boat turned over.'

'I think you're all muddled up, Jamie.'

His small face turned scarlet. 'I'm not all muddled up. That's what Joe said.'

'All right, all right,' she soothed. 'Don't start shouting. All the guests are looking at you. Now what are you going to draw for me?'

'I'm not going to draw you anything,' Jamie muttered, clutching the coloured pens to his

101

chest as he climbed down from the stool. 'I'm going to see what Gran's making in the kitchen.'

Lisa looked at the picture after he'd gone. It really was very good for a five-year-old. He must have some of his father's talent, she decided, remembering the little watercolour of St Michael's Mount that Matthew had given her as a birthday present.

This was quite clearly Wrecker's Cove, with its horseshoe curve and high cliffs in the background. She stared at it more closely, studying what Jamie said was a lantern, as a prickle of uneasiness inched across her shoulder-blades.

A light on the cliffs, exactly where she'd seen one gleaming so many times recently.

I need to tell Matthew, she thought. Now maybe he'll believe me.

But Matthew was already on his way to a remote Greek island, with Stella.

*   *   *

'Seen any more strange lights?' Andy's voice startled her as he came into the bar, shaking raindrops from his black leather jacket.

Would he laugh if she told him?

'Yes,' she said slowly.

His freckled face was serious. 'When?'

'Saturday night. Quite late. After the dance.'

'When all good little girls should have been

fast asleep,' he said.

'There were two lights,' she burst out, glad to have someone to confide in. 'One out to sea, signalling. The other on the cliff, near that huge rock. And look at this.' She produced the coloured drawing. 'Jamie drew it. He says that yellow blob is a lantern and it's a mermaid.'

Andy's flecked brown eyes slanted up at her as he bent to lift a crate of bottles.

'That's right.'

Lisa frowned in puzzlement.

'The mermaid was what they called Joe Trenoweth's lantern because it lured sailors to their doom,' he explained. 'He hung it out on that rock in a storm. And that's why this inn is called the 'Mermaid', after the light. And why the cove is Wreckers' Cove.'

'But the sign hanging outside shows the usual sort of mermaid.'

'That was Matthew's idea. He painted a new board for the 'Mermaid' after he'd renovated the place and taken down the old sign. Nobody would understand, he said. And he was right, wasn't he, seeing the trouble you're having?

'The lantern usually hung above the inn,' Andy went on. 'There's always been a light out there at night to guide the fishing boats in safely—I dare say you've noticed that. In the past, boats relied on it too, and so Joe Trenoweth could be pretty sure of one being wrecked when he moved it to the rock.'

'But that's terrible! Not only was he a

103

wrecker, but a murderer too.'

''Course he wasn't, Lisa. I told you, wrecks were fair plunder. If folk drowned, that wasn't Joe's fault. Not many sailors could swim in those days.'

'But what about the light I've seen out there? What is it? Surely no one's wrecking nowadays?'

'That's for you to find out.' Andy laughed. 'And seeing what a clever sort of girl you are, I don't doubt you will.'

*   *   *

By afternoon the rain turned to a thin drizzle and then ceased, leaving a slight chill in the air. All the resident guests had gone out by then, eager not to miss a day's outing, and only a few local people were in the bar. One was Tom Enys.

'Jamie had a fantastic time at the Aero Park with you and Gwen yesterday, I gather. So how about your evening with Gwen on Saturday?' Lisa asked, perching herself on a stool beside him.

His mouth creased into an irrepressible smile. 'I didn't reckon Gwen would come, m'dear, so 'twas all a bit of a surprise to me when she said yes.'

'She's very fond of you, Tom.'

'Is she?' His weatherbeaten face flushed a darker shade.

Lisa nodded.

'Well, I'd like to ask her out again, but she's always so busy with the inn. It's her whole life.'

'That's to stop her thinking, she says.'

'About Jim, that'd be,' Tom observed with a knowing nod. 'Always a devoted couple, they were. I only wish my life could've been that way.'

'You never married?'

He shook his head regretfully. 'There was a girl . . . 'Twas all a long time ago now. She married another. A baker over by Penzance. But 'tis no use grieving. It happens, m'dear.'

Yes, Lisa thought wistfully, it happens, and her fingers strayed to where Ian's ring had been. He was marrying another, too. Clare.

'Gwen shouldn't still be mourning, Tom,' she insisted. 'It's such a waste of her life. Grief never completely disappears, I realise, but life has to go on—and she's only in her fifties. There's time for her to begin again.'

Tom took a long pull at his glass of cider. ''Tis not an easy thing to do, m'dear. Not when you've been as close as they were.'

'I'm sure you can persuade her,' she said. 'Please try.'

Two lonely people, she thought. Both letting their lives drift by, when things could have been so different.

She saw his eyes suddenly brighten, and Gwen come through the lounge door, hesitating slightly before moving across to join them, a glow lighting up her face.

'Quiet afternoon again, Gwen?' he asked.

She smiled. 'Looks like it, Tom. Everyone's off trying to catch up on the better weather.'

'Then how about coming over to Falmouth with me? 'Twould make a nice drive.'

Seeing Gwen's eager look change to doubt, Lisa said quickly, 'There's no need to worry about the 'Mermaid' or Jamie. I can manage them both quite easily. There'll probably only be a few cream teas to do. Go and enjoy yourself for an hour or two, Gwen. It'll do you good to have a change.'

'Are you sure?'

'Of course I'm sure! I am supposed to be learning how to run an hotel. If I don't get an opportunity to do so on my own, then how am I going to succeed?'

'Well, when you put it like that . . .' Gwen smiled.

'Off you go then,' Lisa said, giving her a gentle push. 'And do remember to take that apron off first.'

*   *   *

Jamie was still in a difficult mood. Whatever Lisa suggested, he didn't want to do and she was beginning to despair until Andy decided she should take him down on the beach for a while.

'The poor kid's been cooped up in here all

106

day, Lisa. I'm not in any hurry to get away, so I'll keep an eye on things. If there's a sudden rush, I'll give you a shout, but from the look of it, the afternoon's going to be a pretty slack one.'

'Just for half an hour then. We'll be back before anyone wants tea. Go and find your bucket, Jamie. There's sure to be lots of treasure washed up after the rough seas.'

CHAPTER EIGHT

The tide's ever such a long way out, Lisa.' Jamie tugged excitedly at her hand, pulling her towards the rocks. 'Can we climb round to the next cove? That's where Daddy and me went and found the seal. We might find another one. And there's a cave. Please, Lisa.'

She shot a cautious glance at the sea. The tide was very low, leaving a wide expanse of flat sand strewn with trails of seaweed and bits of jetsam. It would be ages before it rose again.

'Not for long, Jamie. I promised Andy we'd only be a little while, and it'll be time for tea soon.'

With a shriek of glee, he scampered ahead and began to scramble over the rocks like a little monkey. Lisa followed more slowly, placing her feet carefully, avoiding wet festoons of trailing seaweed and the sharp edges of clinging limpets.

The next cove was only a cleft in the cliff, with sheer sides towering above. Miniature waterfalls trickled down the smooth face of the granite and meandered their way across the sand in little rivulets to reach the sea.

Higher up, bright green ferns grew from small shelves of rock, to catch and hold tiny pools of water, until they brimmed over to continue their downward flow. Rather like a fairy grotto, Lisa reflected.

'Here's the cave,' Jamie shouted, disappearing into a shadowy hole, its entrance heaped deep with storm-tossed seaweed.

*　　　*　　　*

Lisa bent to follow.

Inside it was larger than she imagined, the roof arching upwards, and she was able to stand quite easily, gazing at walls that dripped around her.

There was a clammy throat-catching sort of smell, a mixture of seaweed and dampness, and she peered anxiously down at the grey shingle of the floor, hoping nothing else had died there like the seal.

'There's a tunnel that goes on and on and on, Lisa.' Jamie's voice echoed hollowly and she saw he was already vanishing into the dark gloom at the back of the cave.

'Be careful, Jamie,' she warned, catching up

with him and staring anxiously into the murky dimness of the tunnel. 'This is probably part of the old mines.'

'I know,' he replied. 'Joe said the smugglers used to bring all their treasure here and hide it. Shall we look for some?'

She laughed, hearing the sound travel eerily back to her. 'I doubt they'd leave any behind for you to find, Jamie. Don't go any further. It's much too dark.'

'I can see ever so easily,' he assured her, darting on. 'Carrots make you see in the dark, Gran says, and I eat lots and lots.'

'Well, I obviously haven't eaten enough then,' Lisa protested, bending her head lower. 'So just you come on back here.'

'Look what I've found!' his voice shrieked in the distance, and she stopped, waiting for him to appear again.

What would it be this time? A dead crab? Some glittering piece of rock like those she'd seen up at the disused mine workings near St Agnes? Or some other washed-up scrap of jetsam?

But when he emerged into the murky daylight again, Jamie was clutching a plastic bag.

Mystified, Lisa took it from him, studying the fine white powder that bulged in it. Then, something clicked.

'Whereabouts did you find this, Jamie?' she asked sharply.

'There's a big box. Come and see.' His cold sandy fingers pulled at her hand and she ducked into the tunnel to follow him.

In the half-light, on a ledge part-way up the wall, she saw a small white polystyrene container. One corner had broken away, so that some of the contents had slipped out to fall on the floor. It was full of similar packets.

Modern-day smugglers don't need brandy, fine silks or tobacco, she reflected. There's no money in those any more. This is a far more profitable cargo.

'We'd better hurry back to the 'Mermaid', Jamie, and phone the police to tell them what you've found.'

'Can't we go a bit further, Lisa, to the end of the tunnel?' he pleaded. 'There might be lots more treasure hidden. Real treasure, like silver goblets and rubies, not these silly old plastic bags.'

'No!' she said abruptly. 'We've got to get back.'

The cave had become a frightening place. Whoever put the box there, wouldn't leave it. The contents were far too valuable. He'd come back, and at what better time than low tide?

Fear made her turn quickly to get back to the entrance, a cluster of damp seaweed slithering under her feet. With a cry of pain, she flung out her arms to save herself from falling, fingers sliding down the cold chill of the rock. And then a flame of agony shot through her ankle, searing its way up to her knee.

'What's the matter, Lisa?' Jamie's voice was anxious as she slumped to the ground.

Pressing her hands against the dank stone, she tried to lever herself upwards, only to slide down again, and she bit back another cry before it could burst from her lips. 'I've twisted my foot, Jamie. It's all right. I'll be better in a minute. Just let me sit here quietly for a while until the pain stops.'

'Is it a bad hurt?' he questioned, kneeling down beside her. In the gloom she could see the pale outline of his face, the wide blue eyes staring into hers.

'Just a bit.' She tried to keep her voice steady.

'Shall I rub it better for you?'

'No! Please, Jamie. Don't touch it.' Her voice rose in panic.

He buried his head into her shoulder. 'I don't like you hurting, Lisa.'

'I don't like it either, but it'll be better soon.'

She eased herself into a sitting position, trying to keep her leg still as she did so, feeling splinters of pain shoot through it. Maybe if I crawl, she thought, inching her body forward, and then sank back again with a muffled groan.

'Can you go down to the entrance of the cave and see how far away the sea is?' she asked him after minutes had passed during which the pain only intensified. 'Just to the

111

entrance, Jamie, no further.'

Maybe she could persuade him to climb back over the rocks to the 'Mermaid'. It wasn't difficult. He was always scrambling over them. Andy was at the inn and he'd soon organise a rescue.

She watched the little boy move away, seeing him silhouetted against the gleam of brightness ahead; then heard the splash of his feet.

'I'm all wet now,' he protested, running back to her.

The tide had turned and was racing rapidly across the flatness of the sand, Lisa guessed. It must already have been coming in before they found the cave. Now it had reached the entrance, cutting them off from the next bay. There was no way back.

She glanced along the sides of the tunnel where seaweed and barnacles clung, trying to work out exactly how high the water would reach; and terror crept into her. They had to get out of here. At least nearer the cave entrance, the roof was fairly high.

Maybe she could swim with Jamie? Then the sea would support her. There would be no need to put any weight on her ankle. But would she be able to hold him, or would he be frightened by the incoming swell of the tide and struggle?

There were currents out there, too. She remembered their relentless drag when she'd swum to the rock that day. And how the waves crashed against the sheer smooth face of the cliffs when the tide was high, sending gigantic plumes of spray upward with their force.

What chance would the pair of them have?

Desperately she sank on to her hands and knees once more, dragging herself along, her teeth biting into her lower lip as she felt the shingle grit into her skin.

The floor of the cave was already flooded, each wave pushing a ragged line of debris in through the entrance. Jamie stayed very close beside her, his small face anxious.

'Are you 'tending to be a mermaid, Lisa?'

If only it was all pretend, she wished, and scanned the cave's rough walls to judge how high the sea had reached before. If she could find a ledge well above the tideline . . .

Someone would be searching for them by now. She'd told Andy they'd stay on the beach for only half an hour, no longer. He'd realise something had happened.

Wouldn't he?

Fallen rock piled the sides of the cave, draped by fronds of seaweed, the kind Jamie loved to pop, and she knew soon it would be completely covered. If we could climb right to the top, she thought, there we might just have a chance.

Besides, it couldn't be long before someone found them, she told herself, wanting to believe it.

'Could you climb up there, Jamie?'

Her trembling hand pointed to the rocks.

'Easy-peasy,' he replied, scrabbling his way up. 'Now you.'

Now me, she thought, biting her lip even harder as she began the struggle. Using her one good leg and the knee of the other, she could lever herself from stone to stone, their roughness scraping her skin, the salt and sand stinging.

'I'm the king of the castle,' Jamie chuckled, perching himself at the top. 'I said it was easy-peasy. Look, Lisa, there's lots of sea-anemones in this pool. They all close up when you put your finger in.'

At least he's finding it an adventure, Lisa told herself thankfully, her head finally coming level with his excited face as she flopped exhausted on to the rock beside him.

'Let's 'tend we're seagulls.' He beamed. 'You can be a herring gull. Joe says they're ever so, ever so 'normous. And I'll be . . .'

He wrinkled up his nose while he thought.

'What can I be, Lisa?'

She rested her head against the cave wall, eyes closed, trying to still her shaking body.

'Oh, I don't know. How about a little tern? You know, the ones with pointy sort of wings.'

'Are there bigger terns?' he asked her.

'Probably,' she replied.

'Then I'll be a great big tern.'

'Pretend you're sitting on your nest then,

114

Jamie, and stay very, very still.'

'Seagulls are silly,' he grumbled, after a few minutes had passed. 'Now what shall we do? My hair's getting all wet.' He leaned sideways as water dripped off the roof on to his fair head, darkening it.

'Let's sing some songs,' Lisa suggested, slipping an arm round him and pulling him closer to her side as she felt the splash of a wave drench her foot. 'There'll be a lovely echo in here.'

'Daddy and me do counting songs when we're in the car sometimes. There's "One man went to mow" and "Ten green bottles". We did two hundred and ten men went to mow, I think it was, once.' He wrinkled his nose. 'It was a long, long journey. To see my other Gran. And I kept forgetting which number we'd got to. Daddy didn't though. He knows every number there is. Right up to a million million.'

Matthew would be on his island now. Lying there in the sunshine on some remote beach, the sand white and hot.

With Stella beside him.

Lisa felt tears prickle her eyes. What would he do when he heard about Jamie?

She swallowed hard. Someone *would* rescue them. A helicopter patrolled the cliffs every day. She'd watched it making its way above them so many times, hating the incessant noise. Now she'd welcome it.

But Andy would alert the police when he

115

couldn't find them, and they'd inform the coastguard, and then . . .

But who would think to look in this cave?

'We'll do "Ten green bottles" first,' Jamie said. 'I like that one best.' His little face smiled encouragingly up at her. 'Joe'll come and rescue us soon, Lisa.'

For once she wished Joe was real. Jamie had such faith in him.

The pounding of the waves shook the whole cave, echoing through its dark hollowness, almost drowning Jamie's piping little voice as he began to sing, and Lisa joined in, hugging him tight, fighting back her tears as she tried to keep her own voice from wavering off key.

*   *   *

'Is it tea-time yet?' Jamie sighed, leaning his head into the comfort of her shoulder. 'I'm so hungry. My tummy keeps talking about it.'

She glanced at her watch. Almost five o'clock. They must have been here for nearly two hours. Gwen and Tom should be back by now. Gwen would be frantic. Angry, too, that Lisa had broken her promise to take charge of the 'Mermaid' while she was away.

I should never have gone down to the beach.

Never have let Jamie persuade me to climb over the rocks.

Never entered the cave.

116

Why didn't I realise the tide was already coming in?

I've lived here long enough to know how the sea races in over the flat sand, she thought. It doesn't take much time.

I should have known.

And then, slipping like that. It was so stupid.

If only . . .

It's no good regretting, she told herself firmly. I've got to face facts. If Jamie and I can survive for just a few more hours . . .

A few more hours. Despair swept over her, but her chin jutted determinedly.

Of course they could.

The tide would go down eventually. And then . . .

'I'm cold, Lisa.'

It was cold. The chill of the rock was bad enough, but already the spray of the waves was soaking into them. She licked her lips, tasting the salt, feeling the brush of Jamie's damp hair against her chin.

The sea was swirling strongly into the cave, rising higher up its walls.

'Let's sing some pop songs now, Jamie.'

'Don't want to.' A hint of tearfulness quavered his voice.

'Come on, Jamie,' she urged. 'Remember that one we sang with Daddy on the way home from Marazion? It's still top of the hit parade. How does it go?'

She began croakily, deliberately using the wrong words, hoping to encourage him.

'You're not doing it properly,' he grumbled, joining in, the sound of their voices echoing thinly above the drag of the sea.

The entrance to the cave darkened. She could hear the creak and splash of oars.

'It's Joe, Lisa! Come to rescue us,' Jamie shrieked, pulling away from her arms. 'I knew he would.'

Slowly she lifted her head.

But it wasn't Joe.

It was Matthew.

CHAPTER NINE

Lisa slept for a very long time. When she woke it was night, the room lit only by a soft glow from the bedside lamp. Silhouetted against the faint outline of the window, Matthew sat in a wicker chair.

'You should be on your Greek island,' she whispered, faintly accusing.

He rose to his feet and came to sit on the end of her bed.

'I decided not to go,' he answered. 'There were reasons . . .'

She saw his mouth curve into that teasing smile.

'Maybe I enjoyed your birthday a little too

118

much. So I turned round and drove back here again.'

His hand reached out to smooth the tangled hair from her eyes, twisting a strand of it round one finger, as his voice lowered. 'And found you were missing.

'Andy was going frantic. People were arriving for tea. Half an hour, you'd told him, he said, and he knew you'd keep to that. But I know my son, and what a persistent infant he can be. Wherever you'd gone, it was because of Jamie.

'When you were nowhere to be found in the bay, we searched the village, then one of the fishermen coming down to the beach remembered he'd seen you earlier from his kitchen window, climbing over the rocks. It was a very low tide, he said, so the next cove could be reached. Jamie was always clamouring to go back there. We found a seal once . . . and a cave. I knew then where you'd be.'

The twist of hair sprang away from his fingers as they tensed, settling into a soft curl against her cheek.

'I was terrified, Lisa. For Jamie . . . for you.' His eyes darkened as he looked at her. 'And at that moment I realised just how much I loved you. I suppose I've always known, but never dared to admit it to myself . . . or to you . . . since you first came here.'

He gave a wry smile. 'Love is something I've grown wary about over the years. But with you,

119

it was as if you'd always been there, close to me. As if you were a part of me. I can't explain . . .'

He turned his head to stare into the lamplight, and she could see the anguish that clouded his eyes.

'The currents are so strong around that point. If you'd tried to swim . . .

'The fisherman took me in his boat. We had a job to keep it steady in the pull of the tide, and when we'd rounded the rocks into the next cove the sea was well up, almost covering the entrance to the cave. Every hope I'd had of finding you was shattered . . . And then I heard you singing.'

His mouth curved once more into a smile while his fingers gently followed the line of her cheek to cup her chin, raising her face to his.

'You really must learn the proper words, little mermaid,' he murmured, and then his lips met hers.

*   *   *

When he spoke again, a long while later, golden light was filtering in through the swaying curtains, brightening the room. A bird twittered somewhere in a nearby tree. Waves softly surged over the shore with a gentle sigh of sound.

'I'm going to stay here, at the 'Mermaid',

Lisa. Jamie's right. I can do my drawings here just as easily as in Plymouth. That's what he says, isn't it?'

'But your job . . .?' she began. And Stella, she thought.

'My job,' he echoed. 'Creating characterless, glass-filled town-centre precincts for a prestigious firm of architects? Oh, I know it guarantees me an excellent lifestyle, but money isn't everything, is it, Lisa? I've always wanted to concentrate on restoring and converting some of the beautiful old properties that are going to ruin here in Cornwall. At least then I'll be helping to save part of our heritage for others to enjoy in the years to come.'

He kissed the top of her head, holding her face gently between his hands.

'But that's not all I want, Lisa,' he murmured, his lips moving softly across her skin to find her mouth again.

There was a rattle at the door and Jamie burst in, clutching a teddy bear.

'Is it morning-time yet?' he demanded.

Matthew sighed heavily and bent to pick him up. 'I think, young man, that it's about time you learned to knock before coming into a lady's bedroom.'

*   *   *

Later, Lisa could hear a great deal of activity

121

down in the cove. It tantalised her, until finally she could bear it no longer, and hopped her way across to the window.

The coastguards' Land-Rover and several police cars were gathered at the top of the shingle and outside the inn. It's about that box hidden in the tunnel in the cave, she thought, recalling how she'd told Matthew about it.

A policeman and woman came upstairs to talk to her.

'Can you tell us exactly what you found? It's impossible to get round to the cave at the moment. We'll have to wait until the tide goes down.'

Carefully she described the box. 'Polystyrene,' she said. 'On a ledge half-way along a low tunnel.'

'That's part of the old mine workings,' the man observed. 'One of the disused shafts. Some of them run right down to the sea. Under it, too, in places. We could probably get to it from inland, if only we knew where to start.'

'One corner was broken,' Lisa went on, 'and there were packets inside. A few had fallen and caught on tiny ledges. That's what Jamie found.'

'You guessed what it was, though?'

She nodded.

'There's been a suspicion the stuff was coming in round this part of the coast, but no way of catching anyone,' the man told her.

'With so many little out-of-the-way coves, we can't be watching all of them.'

'There were lights,' she said. 'On the cliff up there and out to sea. I thought someone was signalling.'

'But you didn't report it?' the man asked sharply.

'I thought there was probably a simple explanation, or I was getting carried away by my imagination.'

'Anything unusual is best reported,' he said gently. 'Could save us a great deal of time, you know.'

'I'm sorry.'

'Tide'll be low enough around early afternoon. We'll be back then. No talking about this, though. It's clearly someone local. Don't want to frighten him off, do we?'

'But what about all your cars outside?' she protested. 'The whole village must have seen them coming down the lane.'

'Yes,' he mused, rubbing his chin. 'That could be a problem.'

*　　　*　　　*

'Do you think you could cope with that ankle down in the lounge on a sofa?' Matthew asked her, coming in to see her just before lunch. 'It seems a pity to leave you up here, missing out on all the excitement.'

Lisa's expression was doubtful. 'I'm not sure

I can manage the stairs.'

'No problem,' he grinned, sweeping her up into his arms and carrying her across the room. 'I'll take you down the same way as I brought you up here.'

Outside on the landing he paused, giving her a quizzical look. 'You do realise you're going to have to put up with Jamie's company, don't you? He's been totally lost without you. It's been murder trying to keep him away. Are you sure you still want to go down?'

'Of course I do!' she retorted.

After Gwen had fussed round with cushions to make her comfortable, and Jamie had settled himself on a stool nearby, guarding her anxiously when several of the guests crowded in to hear the story first hand, Lisa noticed the bar was still closed.

'What's happened to Andy?' she asked.

'The wretched lad hasn't turned up yet,' Gwen told her. 'Can you take over, Matthew? It's well past opening time.'

While the lunches were progressing, the coastguard and police returned, adding excitement, as everyone watched them set off from the beach in a couple of powerful little boats.

On their return quite a while later, Andy was with them.

CHAPTER TEN

'Andy?' Lisa's voice was disbelieving. 'He was the one?'

''Fraid so. They caught him along the mine shaft, coming in from the other end,' Matthew told her regretfully, after he'd learned all the details from the police.

'Apparently a boat using a frogman has been regularly dropping stuff into that cave, and Andy then transported it. To him I dare say it was all rather an adventure. I'm not sure he even realised the seriousness of what he was mixed up in. It wasn't as if he took drugs himself.'

Lisa remembered that hazardous journey on his motorbike over the maze of cliff tracks. Andy knew every inch of them. And the mine workings.

'Poor Andy,' she said sadly. 'He always showed great sympathy for the wreckers and smugglers of old. Said they were mostly tinners, like his great-grandfather. Maybe he thought he was carrying on a family tradition.'

She gave Matthew a questioning look. 'He wasn't related to Joe Trenoweth, was he?'

Matthew laughed. 'You never can tell. A number of the old families round here inter-married. And now, how's that foot of yours? What did the doctor say when he called in?'

'Oh, I shall be hopping about very soon, and

back at my desk. If Gwen's prepared to keep me on here,' she added with a worried glance up at him. 'She hasn't said anything yet.'

'Probably too much on cloud nine to even think about your misdeeds.' He smiled.

'Why?'

'Would you believe my dear mother's getting married again?'

'To Tom Enys?' Lisa asked.

'Was it so obvious? I must be blind. I had no idea at all, although seeing her when she returned from Falmouth yesterday afternoon—before she knew about you and Jamie being missing—maybe I should have realised. She was simply radiant. He'd asked her while they were there.'

'Do you mind?'

'Mind? Good heavens, no. I'm delighted for her ... and Tom. He's a nice guy, and she deserves another chance at happiness. After my father died ... it seemed as if her life ceased as well. I wasn't much help at the time either. Rosalyn had left me, and there was Jamie. My mother had a lot to cope with one way and another, and I must have been very selfish. I was doing the final restoration work on the 'Mermaid' and she suggested taking it on. Helston was too full of memories for her. She wanted to get away.'

'You were living in Plymouth then?' Lisa asked.

'Yes, I was living in Plymouth,' he replied.

'Where you met Stella,' she said softly.

'Where eventually I met Stella, who could have been Rosalyn's double,' he agreed ruefully. 'I should have realised, I suppose. At the time she completely knocked me sideways. I couldn't think clearly. And Stella took control of my life. She's a very efficient lady. Quite determined too.'

'Did you love her?' The words were barely a whisper.

Matthew met her gaze levelly. 'For a while I thought I did. Until I realised how like Rosalyn she really is. Stella is only concerned for herself. No one else matters. I was beginning to decide I was fated never to find perfect love, and then . . .'

The teasing smile was back again. 'A mermaid in a cave changed all that,' he said, and then his expression went bleak. 'I really thought I'd lost you and Jamie. The two people who matter more to me than anything, or anyone, in the entire world. I've never known such torment.'

'It's over now,' she whispered softly, raising her face to his.

'Yes, it's over,' he said, kissing her.

*   *   *

'Daddy can read you a story,' Jamie insisted, tugging a heavy volume from one of the shelves and struggling over to her. 'This is a grown-up book, but it has lots and lots of pictures.'

'Who's been reading it to you, Jamie?' Matthew asked, studying the cover. 'It was one of your grandfather's. He was always very interested in the history of this area.'

'One of the ladies readed it to me ever such a long time ago. It was a very rainy day. I was looking at the pictures and she told me all about them.'

'One of the guests?' Matthew asked.

Jamie nodded, climbing onto the sofa and snuggling next to Lisa. 'You read it to Lisa now. There's a picture of Joe.'

He turned the pages rapidly to find it.

Lisa stared down at the black and white drawing of a boy rowing a boat towards a lantern on a rock, surrounded by a storm-lashed sea, her eyes scanning the words accompanying it.

'So old wrecker Joe Trenoweth had a son, also called Joe,' Matthew said, reading them over her shoulder, 'who greatly disapproved of his father's activities. That must have been a bit of a problem for him.'

'And when young Joe saw the 'mermaid' lantern glowing on the rock, he rowed out there in a ferocious storm to extinguish the flame,' Lisa murmured, following down the page.

'Then, on the return journey, the boat overturned and the boy was drowned,'

128

Matthew finished for her.

So it was young Joe, not his villainous father, Lisa mused, who Jamie chose to be his friend, after he'd heard the story.

Imaginary friend, she corrected herself quickly. It had to be all in Jamie's imagination, didn't it? There was no other explanation.

A slight tremor shivered down her spine. She didn't want to think about the other explanation.

'So Joe is only pretend after all, Jamie,' Matthew said, smiling at her worried face. 'You've almost convinced Lisa he's real, you know.'

'Lisa's my real friend, Daddy,' he announced firmly, rubbing his cheek against hers.

Then his expression clouded.

'You won't go away, like Daddy does, will you, Lisa? You will stay here for always. I don't ever want you to go. I love you too much.'

'And so do I, Lisa,' Matthew echoed softly. 'Will you stay with us . . . for always?'

Lisa gazed back into the matching blue of two pairs of eyes, seeing the pleading that filled them, and smiled.

'How could I possibly refuse?'